The Sound

HOWARD BOLING

I0555746

Text Copyright ®2015 Howard Boling

Publishing Copyright ©2015 Laurel Rose Publishing

Laurel Rose Publishing

www.laurelrosepublishing.com

laurelrosepublishing@gmail.com

ISBN-10: 1-944583-06-8
ISBN-13: 978-1-944583-06-4

Acknowledgements

To all of the ones who brought nightmares to my doorsteps, thank you. I have used them well.

Contents

Secrets Kept

Heartbeat still

In skeletal cage

Hands of time

Tied with days

A whisper screaming

Loud its rage

With buttoned lips

From undug graves

Secrets kept

For better days

Where devils walk

And children play

Prologue

The Beniot Family Cemetery

Twenty miles west of New Orleans

November 1818

The dark flesh of the shadows cast by the marble monuments enveloped the desolate figure. Each statue and stone seemed to take audience to the mourning soul, standing near the most recent grave. The sunken holes scattered about the small burial yard slowly filled, as the steady drizzle continued, as it had for the past week.

"All of this..." the words echoed in the man's head, afraid to break the sacred silence of death,

"...in the span of a week."

The man extended his arm allowing his finger tips to brush over the cool, smooth surface of the newly erected cross. Slick from the late autumn rain, he could scarcely make out the one word chiseled into the stone. The family name of Benoit.

Tears streamed down the man's gaunt face as he placed his head against the cross. Unable to control his veiled heartache any longer he collapsed to his knees in the thick mud, sobbing uncontrollably. His blond hair, heavy with rain, hung down, shielding his eyes from the sorrowful sight of his lover's name. His broken cries sent forth a silverish haze, as the warmth of his breath collided with the chill of the night.

Soon, he pulled himself to his feet. He was soaked to his core, his fine frock coat and breeches were covered in a dense layer of greyish mud. A rose that he had brought was now crushed inside of his clenched fist. He slowly opened his hand, looking at the ruined flower and the severed petals, a dark crimson surrounding the rose. The numbing cold repelled the pain from his thorn slashed palm. This reminded him of his life now, ruined and numb.

Once more the tears poured, unwanted, from his grief swollen eyes. He discarded the wasted remains of the rose and attempted, feebly, to straighten his garments, realizing how maniacal he must look. He brushed his stringy hair from his face with his unwounded hand. Trembling, he leaned forward, pressed his lips against the name and dared to whisper a final goodbye.

"Goodbye, my heart," he spoke, in a voice no louder than a sigh.

"I will carry this emptiness with me always, my love. My sorrow will know no end."

With a strained choke of tears, William Bell fled the cemetery, racing to his stolen horse as if he feared that his departed lover may suddenly claw out of the grave for one final embrace. William mounted his horse and spurred it into the chilling downpour of the dark Louisiana night. Withered trees draped in Spanish moss stood along the boundaries of the muddy road like skeletal hands, twisting out of the earth, reminding him of their last night together. The night of the catastrophic dream, which tore through the seams of unconscious reality, but William fought away these thoughts. He had no more time for these cursed memories.

Chapter 1

Near Charlestown Massachusetts

February, 1819

The night had been bone numbing cold, as the many nights before. The oblivion of winter had firmly settled over the land. William Bell sat upon his exhausted mare, staring bleakly into the still valley. His stomach rumbled and his skin was stretched so tightly about him that he considered that his bones may break through. He was starving. He and his mount. His funds had long since ran out and his supplies were nearly gone.

He raised his head, looking into the dark, desolate night. Not even a faint luster of an incandescent star betrayed the shroud of this stygian heaven. Already, he could feel the approach of the sound, tearing at the outskirts of his mind, pounding inside of his skull, demanding his attention. William drew his cloak about him tightly, wishing that this mere piece of tattered cloth could shield him from what was to come.

Then, with the enthusiasm of a criminal being led to the gallows, he gently nudged his tired horse onward. Down the steep path, he guided his mount, his thoughts lingering back on what was lost to him. He didn't dwell on this for long, for the pain had found him. A gasp escaped him as the sudden sensation coursing through his thin body sent him crumpling forward. His long, slender fingers, dry and cracked from the bitter cold, gripped his horse's mane in a weak attempt to stay mounted. Fear flowed through his veins and reasoning vanished, as if it was escaping through his pores, in the disguise of the cold layer of sweat, which now covered his aching frame.

The woods seemed to come alive with dark shadows and shapes, reaching and groping, driving him from the trail. He spurred his horse on faster, hunching over in the saddle and lying close to the once powerful animal. Branches and thorns stung William's face and hands. He felt whelps rising and flesh tearing. Was he screaming? He could not tell over the great, thunderous sound, ringing in his ears.

The horse suddenly came to a halt, neighing wildly and stomping in circles, seeking an escape from the darkness, the madness, and her horror stricken rider. William looked about, eyes wide. His long hair, now torn loose from the small silk ribbon which had held it back, whipped across his face. Among the darkness of the trees, far off in the distance, he could make out a structure, stretching towards the canopy of blackness above, attempting to elude the wraith-like tendrils of the woods. The dim glow from a single shimmering light dared to penetrate the darkness, ever so slightly. A sense of false hope flared inside of William Bell as he glimpsed this beacon.

The jaws of the unknown opened wide and he swore that he could feel the breath of death upon his chill wracked body.

"Yhahh!" he screamed, digging his heels into the panicked horse's sides, driving the terrified beast towards the only possible salvation; the light. The harder he spurred his mount, the more reality seemed to slow, as if the wheels of time would stop entirely, to allow the sound that had plundered his mind for so long now, its chance to violate him once more.

William attempted to scream, but his despair expelled it in a barely audible shriek. He spun back to peer over his shoulder, to chance looking into the haunted woods at his unseen adversary. The blackness turned and twisted in a silent cyclone of horror. The light from the structure was beginning to take form, as his forlorn race carried him closer. The form of a cross! That was the light! A single burning cross of faith, suspended in the wilderness. At the recognition of this holy symbol, the sound seemed to shrink back...away. But William heard a loud tearing as the fabric of his cloak snagged securely upon one of the many low hanging branches. A quick tug and William found himself suspended in the air and in the same timelessness, leaving him to the full realized terror that he was falling.

Shock overtook him as his body crashed against the frozen earth. His breath was forced from his lungs, knocking him senseless, leaving just enough clarity for him to realize that he was slipping into an unwanted state of unconsciousness. He lay still on the hard ground, his gapping eyes fixed upon the fleeting cross, that one, small, beautiful light, slowly being drowned in the swirling blackness.

As the waves of darkness rose up, preparing to break upon his sanity, William Bell heard the roar of the sound, growling as it crashed down upon him, consuming him with nothingness.

Chapter 2

Awakening, almost as if he were trying to escape a childhood fairytale gone mad, William opened his eyes to see what surely, he thought, must be Heaven. Bodiless and free, he spun about. Silver crested clouds, kissed with but a tinge of sunlight extended eternally in all directions. In the distance, an immense structure soared to dizzying heights. Its gold and silver towers seemed entitled to majesty. And the sound?

The only sound, or thought, in this divine sphere of tranquility was an unseen choir of serene voices, emanating from the temple. If he had eyes or tears, he would weep. But now, he was beyond that. Beyond all.

On instinct alone he willed himself towards the source of this beautiful song, this chant of angels. As he neared the tower the brilliance should have been too much to bear, but there was no pain, only the desire to become one with the heavenly light. The song seemed to call to him in a secret language that only he could understand, inviting him into the temple to hold court among those beautiful voices. The glory of this holy structure was more evident as he drew closer. He could make out the intricate details of angelic bodies etched into the golden walls. These images seemed to come to life and move fluidly across the surface of the structure, each swaying gently with the voices.

Then, suddenly, the realization burnt through William Bell, fire through his soul. He did not belong here. These sights were not meant for his eyes, or any others for that matter. His willingness to journey to the tower of gold was abruptly halted, as a foreign presence forced itself into his psyche.

He now felt ashamed that he had desecrated this realm with the filth of his presence. A faint laughter echoed through his mind. So familiar, yet utterly frightening was the only way to describe what was happening. A thought, not his own, trampled through his senses to the front of his mind, demanding his attention.

Words formed in his disembodied intellect.

"God forgives", it hissed, "but do I?"

Then it was gone and with it all sanity. The elegant cloud-like realm, once locked in eternal sunset was now dark and brooding. Clouds swirled angrily, as if promising of a storm to come that could douse the very fires of Hell. The golden temple shook and rattled with the thunderous fury of the storm. The once angel-like figures, carved into the walls, were now horribly distorted, their faces contorted with a combination of hatred and pain. Their mouths, stretched wide in a sickening grimace, exposing long, sharp fangs which curved, pervertedly outward.

These monstrosities seemed to direct their gaze toward William, as if they could see him. The hideous images tore, franticly, at their surroundings in an attempt to rip themselves free from their golden prison.

And the angelic voices that had seemed all encompassing had silenced.

The voices had stopped and all that could be heard was the thunder, reverberating like a thousand horses' hooves. From somewhere far below a great inferno erupted. The angry clouds swirling about the temple's base seemed to ignite as the flames raced upwards in an overwhelming attempt to swallow up the once grand structure. The encompassing flames offered no escape as they leapt up the temple walls, intertwining through the great arching windows, engulfing the tower from outside and within alike and causing the trapped golden demons to howl.

The voices, once synchronized beauty, now joined together for a final performance of pain, as they were consumed by the fire. William tried desperately to look away, to shut his mind to this vision, this abomination, but he could not. He could only watch as the angels within flung themselves from the blackening tower out of flame spitting windows, their celestial wings engulfed in hellfire.

One by one, they plummeted, and for a moment the voice, the sound, was back with William.

"Now," it whispered with the sound of the last breath from a corpse trying to hold to life, "You are cast to a darker Hell."

And with that, the hellish realm began to fade into darkness as William slipped, silently, away with it.

The darkness slowly gave way to light. Shadowed images blurred their way into focus. William looked wearily about his surroundings. He was shivering, burning with fever he could tell, as he gripped the shabby blanket tightly.

"Blankets?" he mumbled to himself as he groggily attempted to make sense of his situation. He struggled to sit up, realizing that he had been laid to rest in someone's bed. The sharp pain in his shoulder jarred his memory back to the fall from his horse. A huge sense of relief flooded over him as he realized that he had survived another battle with this thing that haunted him, yet an intimate feeling of dread remained and there was nothing that he, or anyone, could do about it.

He gazed about the room. A slight movement of his arm forced an audible cry of pain. Memories of his vision slowly poked and prodded, like dull knives, agonizingly, back into his mind. The room was bathed in candle light, radiating from a trio of candles setting upon a table in front of a window, the form of a cross cut into the closed wooden shutters. Could this have been the source of the illuminated symbol that he had so desperately tried to reach before the sound overtook him? The walls of the room were bare, save for a small wooded crucifix and rosary beads, which hung somberly at the head of his bed. His boots were placed at the foot of the bed and his coat and cloak were warming beside a dying fire, which popped and spat in defiance, in a small stone hearth.

The glowing embers made William shiver as images of the fires that scorched his mental Heaven came to mind. He could hear soft steps from outside the old wooden door, the only entrance to his room. The metal hinges gave forth a slight groan as the door was pushed open, slowly.

A dark robed figure glided into the room upon a gust of dank air from the outer chamber.

"Where am I?" William asked, his head pounding, not really wanting an answer, wanting only to fall back into this warm bed and sleep, to try to dream away the pain in his body and mind, to forget the nightmare that his life had become, to not wake up, so that it is safe to forever dream of his lost love without the fear of the specter of death, waiting to take back the happiness that was lost to him when the dream was over.

The figure walked to a small table beside the bed. Whether the robed figure answered his question, he had no idea. The blood pounding in his ears muffled, even, his own voice. William let his eyes follow his unknown visitor, his body too weak and aching to move any longer. The person lifted an earth colored, clay pitcher from the table and began pouring water into a washing basin. The cool, clear water sparkled in the candle light, seeming to dry William's parched mouth further, as he made an effort to speak to the figure again.

"Water...Please..." he rasped through wind chapped lips.

The robed form turned towards him. Candle light penetrated the shadows cast by her garment. William could make out the delicate features of a young woman, enchanting in her simplicity. Her red lips pressed together in a sympathetic smile. A simple olive wood crucifix hung from the young nun's robes.

"An angel..." William mumbled under his breath, his throat raw from unconscious screams.

"No," she replied, "I'm afraid not. I do, however, believe that our Lord guided me to you, perhaps with the aid of angels. It was a miracle in itself that you were heard screaming from those woods. You could have easily frozen to death on these dark nights. When we ventured forth to investigate we found you in the throes of some violent fit, your body shaking and your fever high enough to kill most men. Many would have thought you devil possessed but we here at our convent devote ourselves to the healing of both body and soul. We have seen episodes like you had before, mainly in lunatic asylums. Are you from an asylum, sir?"

"No," William Bell answered softly," Not at all. Convent, did you say?"

"Yes, sir." She replied, "I am Sister Mary Ann. You have found your way to the very steps of our Ursuline Convent."

The nun extended the clay pitcher toward William.

"How did you find yourself so far off of the trail, lost in these woods?" she asked

"I remember nothing." He said, knowing that he could not tell her the truth. He placed his trembling hands upon the cool, water filled container, shaking so violently that the water sloshed around inside the pitcher, threatening to spill, in an attempt to further deny his unquenched thirst.

Sister Mary Ann gently steadied the container with her own hand as William placed his swollen lips upon it. The cold liquid was breath taking as it flooded his dry throat. In his grand attempt to drink the entire contents of the pitcher, the water trickled from his mouth, down his chin and chest, and across his sweat soaked clothes.

William fell back upon the straw stuffed bed. Sister Mary Ann leaned forward and placed a cool, water soaked cloth upon his fevered brow. The sudden sensation caused his body to jolt, involuntarily, as the young woman put her hand upon his forehead in an attempt to comfort him.

"Shhhhh, sir," she said softly to him, "you are very sick and must rest."

William took a deep, struggled breath and released it, letting the fevered sleep of the dying swallow him.

The beautiful voices of the singing angels flooded William Bell's senses with an overwhelming feeling of peace. He turned his head in the void of blackness, searching for the angels...or the splendid temple of gold. Wait...The temple, the angels, they had all been destroyed by fire. Then how could there be these beautiful voices? The very fires of Hell had consumed this Heaven, yet it had somehow survived?

The blackness began to waver and William became quite aware that he was no longer bodiless. He, indeed, had a body and it was, very much, in pain. He could feel the tightness in his chest from the wracking cough that had plagued him for so long now. The muscles of his body seemed to scream in protest as he struggled, feebly, to move. His eyelids were heavy as steel. Too heavy to open, as memories of young Sister Mary Ann crept back to his awareness.

With supreme effort, he managed to open his eyes. The dim candle light was a brutal assault on his senses. He squinted, trying to identify objects hidden in the inky shadows about him. William sat up in his bed, the room slowly coming into focus. The fire in the hearth had been replenished and his clothing was lying as he remembered.

A deep agonized breath escaped him as he moved to the edge of the bed. The cold stone floor sent shockwaves throughout his body when his bare feet made contact. He was now sure that he was awake, but he sound of the angelic choir could still be clearly heard. Groggily, he forced himself to his unsteady feet and carefully navigated his way across the room to where his clothing lay, warming beside the fire. He dressed himself slowly, each movement pure agony. He felt as if he were an old man nearing the end of his life. Wincing, he pulled his boots on his blistered feet and stood, warming his hands by the gentle fire in the fireplace.

The warmth felt good on his battered skin. He could tell that the fever was still with him, but he had no more time to rest. He had wasted too much time here already. He crossed the room to the door and carefully pushed it open. The cool air from within the corridor overtook him and his head began to spin. He stumbled a few steps before placing a hand against a wall to steady himself. William fought away the urge to collapse back into the waiting arms of oblivion. Taking another deep, ragged, breath, he pushed his way down the dark hallway.

The singing grew louder and seemingly even more wonderful. He followed the sound of the voices, blindly, trance-like, almost the same as in his vision. He had to see, for himself, what creatures were capable of such beauty.

"This," he thought, "truly is the sound of angels."

He came to a door which was decorated with ornate carvings of angelic beings and other biblical references, some of which he didn't recognize. The voices seemed as one, as note after wondrous note was completed. He placed his ear to the door. The melody called to him from inside. His trembling hand reached for the door handle and pulled. Light poured out from the door crack, spilling into the dank, dark corridor in an effort to chastise any impurities concealed there.

William, silently, peered into the chamber. Flames atop white candles, too numerous to count, illuminated the worship hall. The smell of incense filled the room, pouring out to William Bell, making him nauseous and overpowering his senses. Inside, the ceiling arched high above the dozen or so black clad women emitting the most magnificent song that he could ever imagine. It was perfect harmony.

William stood in quite amazement as the nuns continued their song, oblivious to their secret onlooker. His heart seemed to stop in its chest when a hand gently touched his back and he froze, his body no longer listening to commands.

"Sir, you should be resting." the female's voice said. Breathing a sigh, he relaxed and softly closed the door. Turning to face her, he replied, "I'm sorry, Sister. I awoke and heard this singing."

"Yes." she responded, "Each morning we gather and sing our praises to our Lord."

William recognized the familiar face from his room.

"Sister," he started in a whisper, "I thank you for the care that has been given to me and I know that this will sound odd however, please, hear me when I say that you and all others within these walls are in the gravest of dangers!"

"What do you mean, Sir?" she responded, her eyes widening and taking a few steps back, concern spreading across her face.

"I mean that I have seen this place…no…one akin to it, in my dreams. I went there and after my arrival it was destroyed and all who dwelled there perished."

"Sir," Sister Mary Ann spoke, "Your fever is high and your dreams are strange because of it. I assure you that there is no danger within these walls, only the protective and healing hands of our blessed Lord."

"I am sorry, Sister." William answered, "I do not share your confidence. I fear that my presence here has already placed you all at risk."

With that, he rushed past the young woman of faith and fled back down the hall from which he came.

"Please, Sister," he called back over his shoulder, "do not make light of my warnings!"

William ran, blindly, through the long, candle lit hallways searching for an exit to the outside. Rounding a corner, he saw, at the end of a short foyer, a large set of double oak doors, barred by a heavy wooded beam. Using all of the strength that he could muster from his frail frame, William placed his weight beneath one side, managing to topple the wooden barrier from its securing brackets.

The crashing weight of the beam striking the stone floor resounded throughout the corridor, a haunting remembrance of the bellowing thunder preceding the firestorm from his dream. Placing his shaking hands on the massive handles, William swung open the heavy doors and was hit by the bitter cold of the predawn morning. The dry air took his breath away and he gasped at the sensation.

Gathering his wits, he saw to his left, that his horse stood tied to a knotted fence and eating from a hanging bucket, in an area across the way. Still saddled, the animal seemed calm and rested, something William envied, as he felt neither calm nor rested. He hastily crossed the frosted ground toward his horse, wondering to himself just how long he had been at this place? He was a beacon of disaster, calling to an unseen horror, and he had to get as far away from here as fast as possible.

The chill of the morning air assaulting him, he felt as if thousands of white hot needles were pricking his weather beaten skin. Each agonized step carried him, faster, to his mount. He quickly untied the reins securing the animal. His breath escaped his body in broken clouds as he carefully mounted the beast. Turning in the saddle, he looked back to the looming structure of the convent. The blackness of the woods beckoned to him with both promises of death and salvation. He nudged his horse towards the trail that had earlier seemed to him to be crafted of stepping stones leading to destruction. He could make out the lone figure of Sister Mary Ann standing, silhouetted, by the inviting candle light from inside. She raised a hand in a farewell gesture. William Bell responded in kind.

"The stepping stones of destruction, indeed," he muttered under his breath as he could feel the numbing spur of the sound scratching inside of his skull, "and the path ends with me."

With that, William Bell dug his heels into his mount's sides, driving it on.

The race for sanity was on again as he disappeared into the timeless gloom of the dark forest.

Chapter 3

Sister Mary Ann watched, concerned, from the doorway as the strange, disturbed, young man became one with the dark shadows of the woods. She shivered beneath her heavy gowns in the doorway of the convent, not sure if from the cold morning air or the pleading seriousness with which the young man had spoken his eerie warning. Reaching out across the entrance threshold she grasped one of the massive doors and pulled, forcing a great groan from the worn hinges as it swung close. As she brought the other door to, the faint, soft, shuffle of feet dragging over the stone floor betrayed the approach of a fellow Sister.

"Sister Mary Ann?" a familiar voice called to her, concern evident in the tone. "You seem troubled. Are you well?"

Sister Mary Ann smiled. That voice, how easily it calmed her now, just as it had in the past. She turned to face her friend and mentor; Sister Agnes.

"The young man that was found days ago, he just took his leave." Sister Mary Ann said, worried.

"He was well enough to depart?" Sister Agnes asked "It is a miracle in and of itself that he is alive. He seemed at death's door but yesterday."

"He is not well enough by any means. Not in good health at all." Sister Mary Ann stated. "He awoke this morning and saw himself out, stammering on about danger on his heels, visions in dreams, and warning that all within our walls were at risk. And to further speak of his dreams, while I cared for him and he slept those days in his fevered state, he rambled on about Heaven and angel and the ravages of hellfire."

Sister Agnes, seemingly deep in thought, leaned and grasped the thick wooden beam on the floor. Sister Mary Ann, her mind returning from her haunted recollection, moved to help the old nun in heaving the beam into its bronze holding brackets, securing the double doors. Turning to Sister Mary Ann, Sister Agnes spoke.

"I suspect that only our Lord can help such a poor, lost, wretch such as he. I also feel that we do well ourselves with his departure. For with it, our own safety has been attained."

Forcing a sympathetic smile to Sister Mary Ann, Agnes could see the inner turmoil of, perhaps, not serving a fellow human to the upmost of her capabilities upon the young nun's face.

"You have done all that could be done." She reassured Mary Ann. "Go, now, and sound the bell for morning Angelus."

Sister Mary Ann nodded, attempting to push thoughts of the troubled young man from her head. She made her way to the entrance of the bell tower to begin her climb up the old wooden stairwell.

Elsewhere in the building, a young novitiate, Sister Christina, made her way into the empty chapel are to light candles, as she did every morning to prepare for personal prayers and meditation. However, when she entered the chapel this morning, something was different. A faint smell of rose petals overshadowed the smallest hint of decay. The smell of a funeral hung heavy in the air. But there had been no deaths or funerals here since last spring, with the passing of one of the elder Sisters. Now, in the very heart of winter, there were no fresh roses to be found.

She walked deeper into the chapel, towards the candelabras near the altar. Her own candle, that she carried, flickered in the darkness, disclosing strange shapes and casting solemn shadowed emotion on the faces of the angelic statues standing on either side of the alter, waiting it seemed, for a silent cue. The woman stopped, a bit ashamed for letting her mind wander like a child's, for actually thinking that her God would allow anything, with evil intent, within these hallowed halls. She smiled to herself as she reprimanded her childlike thoughts and continued towards the altar. Before completing a full step, she detected a slight movement just before the chantry. Startled, her candle dropped from her hand. It, stubbornly, remained ignited as it impacted the floor and rolled towards the altar.

The defiant little flame revealed the kneeling form of a willowy, young woman before the worship table, her back to the surprised nun. A gasp escaped the young novitiate, as the woman, without turning to face her, reached back for the candle. With one graceful motion, she picked up the candle and passed it over three more, standing in their holders on the altar, igniting them. A pale light saturated the room and Sister Christina trembled beneath her robes, as she stood behind the stranger who was silently kneeling.

The candle light danced on her raven colored hair, which hung long down her back. She wore a long, fully sleeved, red dress, trimmed with golden hued threads upon her pale, near skeletal body. Her attire was some of the finest that she had ever seen, but very out of place here in this convent deep in the woods.

Where did this person come from? How did she gain entrance to the chapel? What was her purpose here? A relative, perhaps? A wife or sister to the poor soul found in the woods, here to claim him and take him home?

"Are you well, my lady?" she asked meekly, noting how thin and sickly the young woman looked.

"There is much darkness resting behind these eyes, Sister." Was the cold response from a voice that seemed strained.

"What darkness do you speak of?" Sister Christina continued, slowly closing the distance between herself and the strange woman.

"I speak of betrayal," she began. "Betrayal of flesh and soul, betrayal of friends and loved ones, betrayal of God and nature... Betrayal of myself." She growled, bowing her head in death-like silence.

Sister Christina now stood directly behind the kneeling woman. She placed a hand, gently, upon the young woman's boney shoulder. In a comforting attempt she spoke softly, "So much pain and hate."

"Yes, dear lady," she whispered back, just loud enough for Sister Christina to hear, "But pain and hate have betrayed me not!" Her voice turned to a snarl!

Her movements were so swift that blood was already rising in Sister Christina's throat before she realized that the object protruding from her abdomen was the hilt of a sickle and its curved blade, buried deep in her belly. The young woman, her face still obscured by shadows, stood before the mortally wounded Sister. Sister Christina's arms grasped the stranger's shoulders, as she struggled to stand. The smell of decay was heavy on the stranger's breath. Sister Christina stared, wide eyed, into the shadowy void where the strange woman's face should be. She tried to speak to her, but even as her lips motioned the words she was strangling on her own blood.

A smile spread on the ghostly woman's rotting face, a smile known only to her. Sister Christina slid down her attacker's body, to the cold, hard, floor, her last bit of life fading. The stranger turned, as the dying woman's blood pooled around her. She stepped to the altar and extinguished the candles with a pinch of her fingers, allowing the darkness to swallow up the horrific events that had just taken place. Still smiling, she stepped over the dead woman and vanished into the shadows of the convent, with deadly intent and bloody sickle in hand.

"The bell should have sounded by this time." Sister Agnes said, more to herself than to her young companion.

"She was not in her quarters? Nothing seemed amiss there?" Agnes continued.

"No," replied the novitiate, "Is something wrong?"

"Sister Mary Ann had an encounter with the fellow that was found in the woods. His ramblings were those of a lunatic and deeply disturbed her. I assured her that all was well, however I sensed that she was still troubled." said Sister Agnes.

"I think, perhaps, we should assemble the others and address this situation, to make them aware, as to keep a watchful eye, in the event that the stranger returns with malicious intent. But, first we must find Sister Mary Ann."

The two women now stood at the stairwell leading up to the bell tower. Sister Agnes leaned into the square structure and peered up into the dark tower. The silence remained unbroken.

"Sister Mary Ann?" she called, her voice echoing up into the tower.

"Sister?" she called again.

Silence was the only response. Sister Agnes looked to her companion.

"Come, let us check the tower."

Sister Sadie spoke to Agnes as they stood before the stairway.

"Perhaps she fell ill? I'm sure her reasons are justified."

Agnes took a candle from the hallway and the two nuns began their climb towards the top. Flight after flight of aged wooden stairs groaned and creaked angrily under the women's combined weight, as if threatening to topple them to the ground below. Sister Sadie gripped the wooden rail nervously, her fear of heights making her legs feel as if they were heavy as lead. After long minutes, the two stepped into a small room at the top of the stairwell. Sister Sadie marveled at the endurance of the robust, elderly, Sister Agnes, her round face flush from the climb. Sister Agnes was not a small woman, short and stocky, a figure to be respected, if not intimidated by. She showed strength from decades of independence.

Sadie was still used to being cared for and she missed her family tremendously. This had always been her dream, her way, she had thought. She had come to the convent just over a year ago, yet several times throughout the past weeks, she found herself wavering in doubt. Could she really live out the rest of her life, a recluse from the outside world? Could she? Would she?

Most of the others seemed so sure, so confident, so content, but most of them were twice her age. She was so young, with so many desires that could not be fulfilled within the walls of this convent. Was this really the life that she wanted? Wasn't it too late to change her mind now? Would her family be disgraced?

Her family, how she missed her mother's hugs... And her father, she remembered well the tears of pride as they swelled in his eyes when she left. Her parents were poor and that was how she grew up. Here in the convent she would have a simple life, not the struggles that her family was burdened with. Yet she still wondered, "What is comfort if you give up happiness to attain it?"

"Child?" Sister Agnes repeated, bringing Sister Sadie out of her thoughts.

"I apologize, Sister Agnes," Sadie replied, "my mind has been drifting as of late."

"I understand, dear girl," Agnes answered, "If you ever feel the need, I always have an ear for you."

Sister Agnes stepped to the wooden door that led out to the bell. Pushing open the door, the two women stepped out onto the landing that composed the topmost level of the bell tower. The sky was a wash of dark, greyish blues that was sparsely littered with faint, glimmering stars. The forest that always had towered over Sadie was now far below. The evergreens, black in the pre-dawn, seemed like ocean waves, reaching out to the horizon. A muffled sound of thunder and a flash of lightning, briefly breaking the darkness, warned of the coming storm.

"Dear God!" Sister Agnes gasped as she reached and gripped Sadie's wrist. Sadie winced as she turned to look at Agnes. The old nun's gaze was locked on the form of the large, brass bell which was partially hidden by shadows.

"What is it?" Sadie whispered, but Agnes was already dragging her back towards the door which led to the stairs. Glancing over her shoulder, Sadie could scarcely make out from the distant flash of lightning, Sister Mary Ann; her body hanging by the neck, dangling against the brass bell.

Sadie screamed, horror echoing over the woods as Sister Agnes led her in the descent of the stairs. Paralyzing fear gripped the young woman's body as Sister Agnes dragged her to safety. Sadie's mind raced, trying to make sense of this nightmare as she collided with Sister Agnes, who had come to a sudden halt on the stairs in front of her.

"Sister Agnes?!" Sadie started, tears of fear streaming down her cheeks, "Why are we stopping?! We must get to the others!"

"Hold on, child." Sister Agnes responded grimly.

"What? Why?" Sadie sobbed.

Peering over the stair railing, she could see the orange glimmer of a makeshift torch. The figure carrying it, a woman, strode back and forth as she busily worked. Her dark hair flew about her head, attempting to keep up with her hurried movements. The gold trimming of her red dress shimmered in the torch light.

"Who?" Sadie asked in a broken cry, "Who is that?"

"I don't know, child." Sister Agnes breathed.

The figure moved towards the door which led away from the tower, peering up towards the two women, before tossing the torch beneath the stairs.

"What ills your flesh is heir to!" she wailed, forcing air over dead vocal cords, as the bottom of the stairway exploded in flames.

"Saints preserve us!" Agnes gasped as the intruder sank back into the corridor, passing a small barrel, which once contained oils, its contents now serving as the fuel feeding the flames that were quickly devouring the old tower. Seeing the fear on Sadie's face, Agnes turned her around.

"Back to the top, child!" she exclaimed.

The two women raced back up the stairs to the tower top, struggling to breathe over the thick smoke that was rising up, attempting to escape the tower, turned chimney. The heat was growing more intense with each passing moment, each rasping breath. Finally, they burst out into the fresh morning air. The slightest tint of red was breaking over the skyline, coloring the storm clouds with an anguished tint.

The wind had picked up and whipped at their robes, the ends fluttering about wildly. A loud tapping caught the women's attention. Turning towards the bell, they could make out the badly beaten face of their dead friend, her eyes half open in a sickening stare, her last horrible moments frozen on her face. The wind rocked the heavy bell, though not enough to sound it. In Sister Mary Ann's dead hand, she clutched her wooden crucifix with such force that it had cut into her flesh, leaving blood to stream down the cross and rosary beads, accumulating in a puddle beneath the bell. As the wind gusted, the end of the crucifix clanked against the brass surface as if, in death, Sister Mary Ann was attempting to complete her final duties by sounding the bell.

Sister Sadie now had her arms wrapped about Sister Agnes, hugging her like a frightened child would hold her mother. Tears rolled, hot, down her cheeks. They ran as one, to the edge of the tower. Far below they could see the other sisters fleeing the doomed structure as flames threatened to consume the remainder of the convent.

"There is no way down!" shrieked Sadie, screaming for help that would never come. The other sisters below looked on helplessly. Some were praying, some denying, and some mourning already for those soon to die. A great drop of rain, carried by the bellowing wind, struck Sister Agnes on the cheek. The storm was near. In the distance, rain fell in great sheets, moving slowly towards the trapped women.

"Take care, little Sister." Agnes whispered to Sadie, "Now is not the time to lose one's faith."

Sadie, whose face was buried in Agnes's robe sobbed wildly.

"Perhaps our Lord will save us yet!" The old nun declared.

Sadie looked up from Agnes's robe and gazed towards the salvation that the old woman pointed towards. Turning back to the doorway, Sadie could see the bright orange glow of the fire through the thick smoke, as it pushed ever onwards. The flames now licked about the outer walls, escaping the wooden prison. Sister Sadie dropped to her knees and brought her crucifix to her lips. Kissing the holy item, she spoke her final prayer.

"Please, God, deliver us! I don't want to die! Please!" she begged.

Sister Agnes looked down at Sadie as tears rose in her own eyes. No showing of desperation on her face, Agnes smiled and embraced Sadie.

Far off in the down pour, deep in the forest, William Bell could see thick clouds of smoke spiraling skyward from some distance behind him. He guided his horse towards a clearing, overlooking the valley where the convent stood. Hoping against hope he peered into the valley, finding his nightmare manifested in reality. The convent was enveloped in flames and the bell tower was now a swirling inferno, as the fire consumed it on all sides.

William watched powerless. One figure, engulfed in fire, dove from the tower top in a final attempt to escape. Another followed moments later, as the flames swallowed the tower entirely. William closed his eyes tightly, lifting his face to the heavens as the rain beat down, mingling with his tears.

For a moment the presence was with him and he swore he could hear laughter.

Chapter 4

November 1818

Twenty miles outside of New Orleans, on the banks of the Mississippi River.

A broken old man sat alone in a darkened room at a banquet table within the walls of a grand mansion, sitting on the grounds of a large sugar cane plantation. His balding head rested in his hands as he poured over memories of times, long past. Good memories. The types of memories that should make a good life, but those memories seemed pale in comparison to the losses that had befallen his family and him.

The old man lifted his head and let his eyes wander about the spacious dinning hall, coming to rest on a portrait of his beloved wife. What joys and celebrations had this room been privy to when she was still alive. Those times were gone now. He thought about his home and its history. This plantation was established and built by his family nearly as soon as they had arrived in this land. His parents, long since passed from this world, had left him the sole heir to their vast fortune while he was still in his early twenties.

He rested a hand on the hilt of his saber. It was a feeling that was like instinct to him. This sword had been with him on countless military actions during his youth. He was a soldier, his last engagement being four years prior, not far from his home. On that cold December night, the British took nearly twice the number of casualties during the battle. Even more, the old man mused, had General Jackson not pulled his forces back.

The old man stood up with tears in his eyes. He still wore his ceremonial uniform from the day's events. He had buried his only daughter this day. The tears fell down his weather beaten face as he walked across the dimly lit room to a window overlooking his estate. His body, once powerful and impressive, was now starting to fail him as time marched on. He ached from the day's events and numerous wounds from countless battles, each one a trophy, a testimony of his bravery, his fighting spirit and will to survive. But just as his body was now failing with time, so was his will to live. This esteemed manor now seemed much larger than it ever had and infinitely more empty. Empty of people he loved and full of ghosts, ghosts from his haunted heart. His beloved wife, Lida, had died some years earlier, after a long suffered illness. He remembered watching her in her private chamber upstairs, as she slowly withered away to nothing, slipping away right before him and his children. How powerless he had felt, much like today. On the battle field, he had fought with honor and valor, saving many lives and displaying brilliant leadership, but for all of his courageous deeds, his reward was to wait, powerless, at his wife's side, as she slowly drifted away.

The death of his wife was a crushing blow, worse than any received in battle. Her absence left him to raise their three children on his own. His oldest children, both sons, grew to be hulking men like he was in his youth. They followed in his footsteps, becoming respected soldiers. The old man swelled with pride as he remembered them fighting at his side on that cold December night, four years past.

Then there was beautiful Isabella, his only daughter, an exact image of his loving wife, when she was young. Isabela was the perfect soft balance for this hardened old soldier. She doted on her father when her mother yet lived, but seemed to grow distant and resentful of him after her passing. No matter, he loved her with no measure. The old man loved his sons, but Isabela made it seem that his wife was not gone at all. With her long raven hair and milky pale skin, her infectious laughter, her slightly turned up nose, she glided through these halls giving light to what should have been the darkest of times. Isabella gave him reason to go on.

Where his sons were only happy following in his warrior footsteps, Isabella was content in her study, curled up beside the fireplace reading a book of poetry. She loved art and painting as her mother did. Her singing often echoed through the lonely manor halls. Such a dreamer she was. He remembered arguing with her, halfheartedly, stating, "If reading is such a passion of yours, why not make your studies of something useful, instead of these so called 'arts'."

The look on her childlike face had caused him to smile in spite of himself. Her red lips pouted, jaw clenched tight, the fire in her brown eyes, all so reminded him of his deceased wife.

How he wished he could turn back the hands of time. There was so much he would say, so much he would do differently. He only wanted his children to have a good life, to protect them, but he had failed. And his failure was not to be accepted.

"Father?" a deep voice roused him from his tortured thoughts. Raising a hand to his eyes, he wiped away the tears that betrayed his weakness. He straightened his body and turned to face his eldest son. He stood in silence, inspecting his boy. His frame well over six feet in height and supported nearly twice the muscle mass of an average man. The son stood across the room from his father, shoulders square, arms straight beside his powerful body, his chin held high as if standing at attention, awaiting inspection. He was quite a specimen.

Even in his sorrow, the old man couldn't help but smile.

"Brusion, my son," he spoke in a soft voice, as he crossed the room to stand before the young man. "Your sister lies in her grave this night."

"Yes, father, I..." he started, his words cut off by his father, whose voice suddenly rose to a thunderous bellow.

"And the devil that placed her there still walks free, breathing air that should be filling her lungs!"

Brusion Benoit flinched at the old man's fury.

"Promise me, on your mother's honor, that if you must pursue this fiend to the ends of Hell, you will avenge your sister....my daughter...my Isabella..." the old man trailed off, shaking with grief.

Clinching his jaws, Brusion looked into his father's pain filled eyes.

"Father," he spoke, "I have the servants preparing my supplies even as we speak. I leave at first light and I swear to you, on my mother and sister's graves, that I will end his miserable life."

The old man stood there, his mouth open, wanting to say something but knowing full and well that everything had already been said. Placing a trembling hand on each of his son's broad shoulders, the old man nodded and briskly left the dining hall on his way to check in on his other son, Jacob, who was seriously injured during the day's events.

Brusion started across the room, his powerful stride taking him to the large arching window that overlooked the family cemetery. By the moonlight, he gazed at the mound of muddy earth, marking his sister's freshly filled grave. He reached inside of his vest and removed a small swath of fabric, inspecting it. This tattered piece of cloth was found clutched in his dead sister's hand with the faintest stain of blood upon it.

"Isabella." He sighed, staring at the stained cloth, thinking thoughts of summer days long ago, thinking of Jacob, Isabella, and himself running through the fields of the plantation, playing in the maze like garden area behind his home, listening to her silly stories and suffering through her reading of poetry. He so loved his little sister. Those days seemed just yesterday, but years had passed since the days of their carefree childhood, days that were lost in the strides of time. Now his dear sister was gone from this world. Poor Isabella had been found beaten to death, her body tossed onto the muddy banks of the Mississippi River near the port of New Orleans, so very far from her home and her family that loved her.

He wondered how long she had suffered? How long did she survive? Begging for help? Begging for her life? Screaming? He wondered had she called out for him, during her final moments? Brusion had always been her "protector". How long did she lay in the freezing, flowing water, waiting for death to take her?

Brusion raised his stare from the cloth and peered out the window into the dark night. The cloth was a piece of a cloak that he knew well. It belonged to the brilliant young tutor that had come to live with his family, to further educate Isabella, without her going away to a seminary. This was the common ground that his father and Isabel had reached. She had dreams of going to a female academy in Litchfield, Connecticut, but his father could not bear the thought of his little girl so far from home. This tutor came into their home and poisoned his sister's thoughts, manipulated her, and turned her against her family. Then he took her life. Brusion knew this in his heart. This "tutor" was responsible for all of this and somewhere out there, he still breathed air, polluting this world with his vile existence. He was out there, unpunished.

The name burned on Brusion's lips.

"William Bell," he spoke through gritted teeth, "enjoy the days that you have left, for they are soon to come to an end."

Brusion placed the cloth back inside of his vest, just over his heart. Turning, he left the dining hall to prepare for the coming hunt.

Early the next morning after his son, Brusion, had departed but before the sun had climbed to chase away the pre-dawn gloom, the patriarch of the Benoit family found himself on the grounds of his estate, wandering past the spots where his children once played, approaching the path leading to his loved ones final resting places. He wanted to talk with Isabella, to apologize again for failing her. The old man let his tears fall, unashamed now. His daughter was gone, never to be held in his arms again. How could this be? The old man buried his face in his hands as he walked the familiar path. Wiping his eyes, he peered into the shadowed burial yard. The sight awaiting him could not be real. He wiped his eyes again as he approached his daughter's final resting place. An open grave, where she was buried yesterday, awaited him. Rushing to the edge, he looked, his eyes wide with horror, down into the muddy earth. There was Isabella's empty coffin, filled with mud and rain, the broken lid propped against the grave wall. There seemed to be claw marks at the foot of the grave as if someone had pulled themselves from the earthen prison. A tightness seized the old man's chest as he fell to his knees in the morning muck clutching his broken heart.

Chapter 5

February 1819

William Bell made his way down the muddy trail, mounted on his steed who walked along as exhausted as its rider. The rain had stopped and through the tangled ceiling of branches above he could make out the blue afternoon sky, a sight that seemed scarcely to exist anymore. Over the past weeks thick blankets of grey clouds blocked out the sun nearly every day forcing gloom upon the world. Even the cold of winter seemed to be lost in the unseasonable warmth of this spring-like day. With the gentle rocking of his body mimicking the movements of his horse, William found himself fighting sleep.

Sleep...this was something that he only experienced in small slices now, afraid to close his eyes, afraid of the nightmares that filled his dreams. His head grew heavy, bobbling about, his eyelids drooping. It had been days since he had last slept for more than a few moments and this warm weather beckoned to him, like a favorite blanket to a tired child. William closed his eyes and his mind began to drift.

His thoughts touched briefly on the doomed convent and the merciful, godly women who dwelled within its walls. He put the weight of their deaths on his conscience, for he had led death to their doorstep. No matter how unwittingly, it was his fault. There was nowhere he could turn now, nowhere that death would not follow. Any soul that would dare to help him would have the same fate befall them that befell the women at the convent. Death was stalking him...and it was getting closer.

Memories of Isabella's funeral haunted him. Knowing that he was not welcome he had hidden behind a large marble tomb, watching the mourners gather round a gaping hole in the muddy earth. Isabella's father, wearing his military uniform, complete with decorations and saber, stood flanked by his brawny sons, each dressed similar to their father. The three men stood there, pride forcing back tears of sorrow, or perhaps their tears were mixed with the drizzling rain. He couldn't tell.

As the bearers of the coffin approached, sloshing through the muddied burial ground, audible sobs erupted from those in the crowd of mourners. Isabella was well loved by all and so young, not yet twenty. It was impossible for some to comprehend that such a bright light as she had been extinguished and in such a terrible manner made it all the more tragic. William could not imagine that he would never again engage this beautiful young woman, with her infectious laughter, in hours of conversation and debates, be it politics, the arts, or any number of subjects. He would never look into her beautiful eyes. He would never kiss her soft lips again.

Isabella's coffin was of the finest that money could buy, crafted from the best cherry wood and stained to a dark brown, adorned with a small window in which to view the body. The men carrying the coffin came to a stop and with care, eased it to the slick ground at the side of the open grave. William shook himself from this nightmarish state, unsteadily stepping from behind his hiding place and towards the crowd of mourners. The blood in his body seemed to drain as he neared the sarcophagus which held his young lover. Pushing through the mourners, his chest heaving, producing broken cries, he came to stand at the head of the coffin. Falling to one knee and shaking, he collapsed upon the rain beaten, cherry wood lid, peering through the small glass window at the dead girl inside. Her skin was pale with death, her body well preserved, from the winter cold, given the amount of time that she had been dead. Her dark hair framed her lovely face, still somewhat swollen from her demise. It appeared that she could, very well, just be sleeping in her red dress with golden trim. Grief overtook him and he pleaded for the dead to come back.

Mere feet away, the patriarch of the Benoit family shook with unbridled rage, his mouth wide in disbelief. The very man who was responsible for his dear daughter's demise was here, disgracing her in death, as he had done in life. The old man lunged forward, drawing his sabre, its blade slicing through the cold air. The mourner's shrieks were the only thing that saved William Bell that day, alerting him of the attack and causing him to flinch, the blade whipping by his head and biting deep into the coffin top, the impact cracking the glass window. A boot from the old man struck William squarely in the face, sending him toppling backwards onto the coffin. Cursing William, the old man struggled desperately to free his saber from the coffin lid.

Sitting up, dazed, William could see the mourners retreating from the cemetery, seeking safety from this battle among the dead. William pushed himself off of the coffin attempting to escape, but Isabella's brother, Jacob, was hurtling at him. Jacob's sizable body slammed against

William, sending them both careening backwards. The two men tumbled over the coffin and plummeted head first into Isabella's awaiting grave.

The coffin slid on the muddy earth during the struggle, leaving it teetering dangerously on the grave's edge. In the deep hole below, William felt a vice like grip at the back of his neck. His face was pressed down into the puddled water in the grave's bottom. Thick mud filled his nostrils and mouth as his face struck the floor of the grave. William struggled against the suffocating grip, held by the younger Benoit brother, but to no avail. Jacob was bigger, stronger, and leverage was on his side. William's struggles grew weaker. His lungs burned. Just one breath and this nightmare would be over. Just one breath, already in the grave. Blood pounded in his ears. Far off, William heard what sounded like a screamed warning followed by a muffled crash. Then he was free of the iron like grip. He pushed his face out of the mud, gasping loudly, sucking in as much air as he could, choking and spitting, the taste of the grave in his mouth. He turned to see Jacob pinned beneath one end of Isabella's coffin which had tumbled in on top of them. The dead girl's face was pressed against the cracked window in the lid. Her lifeless eyes, half open, seemed to stare at him from within the coffin. Isabela had saved him from his fate.

Isabella's father and eldest brother, Brusion, strained under the weight of the coffin, which still bore the old man's sword embedded in the lid. Jacob writhed in agony, attempting to shift the weight, his legs twisted and broken, were trapped beneath it. Gathering his senses, William jumped to his feet and clawed his way out of the muddy grave. Fueled by adrenaline he sprinted through the tomb stones, glancing back to see the murderous glare of Isabella's father as he and Brusion dragged the coffin to the side, freeing Jacob, who was howling in pain.

Mourners were now rushing back to aid the Benoits as the old man barked orders.
"Catch that murderer!" he yelled, his voice echoing through the burial yard, "Catch that bastard!"

William Bell's eyes widened in horror.

"'Murderer?!" he screamed, "I've murdered no one!"

A mob of angry faces were now in pursuit. William darted through the monuments, outrunning the hostile mob and vanishing into the woods of the surrounding countryside, the same woods that he had walked with his Isabella. Her face, staring from within the coffin, tore at his soul. When he pulled himself from her grave, he swore that she was smiling at him.

A sudden jostle awoke William from his brief slumber. He had dreamed of the funeral again.

"Isabella," he muttered, looking up to the twilight sky overhead. "You haunt my thoughts, waking and asleep. How am I to keep my sanity?"

A deep pounding at the base of his skull shook his thoughts, almost as if to answer. The sound was back...and it was drawing closer. William reached forward, gripping the reins of his horse and dug his heels into the ribs of the tired creature. His race was on again.

Chapter 6

Running and running, he had no idea for how long. If this had been real, his lungs would have ruptured long ago. But how could it not be real? He could feel the painful blisters on his feet, the combination of sweat and blood as his raw flesh rubbed again and again against the leather inside of his boots. Stride after stride brought him closer to salvation and deeper into madness. The shadowy, thorn filled woods tortured his skin, as it ripped and tore it in seemingly a hundred different directions. Ahead in the distance, William Bell could hear voices. Vaguely, he could hear the voices of children.

Then the woods were gone, as if they had never been and William stood within the shadow of a large church upon a high hill which overlooked a small village. The tiny community seemed deserted, save for two small children whom were setting upon the steps of the church. William approached the children, a boy and girl. The boy looked up as William drew near, his piercing blue eyes, red from weeping.

"What's the matter, child?" William asked in concern.

The small girl with honey golden hair, looked up.

"We are just not ready to say goodbye, sir." She said, her lips quivering.

William looked towards the church doors which stood partially open and could see people filling the pews. At the end of the aisle an open coffin was setting before the altar.

"Someone that you love?" William asked.

The little boy responded in choked words, "Yes and we don't understand how we are supposed to let go."

"Loss is never easy, children," William stated, knowing full well that he, himself, had yet to let go of his loss. He forced a smile as he continued, "I have seen too many that I love pass from this world and I also am unsure as to how to let them go. Perhaps saying goodbye would allow a final word with your loved one. It may seem too little now, children, but you will look back with regret if you do not. Me? I believe that when you speak to those you love, the ones that have gone on before us, that they can hear you. I truly do."

The little girl turned to her brother.

"Should we say goodbye, brother?" she asked sadly.

Looking to his sister the boy solemnly nodded. The children stood and turned to enter the church. The boy paused at the doorway and turned back to William.

"Will you pay your respects also sir?" he asked.

"Please, sir?" the girl added.

Feeling a bit odd at not knowing the deceased, William reluctantly spoke, "Yes, child, I'll join you."

Forcing a smile at the girl, William took the children's hands and they entered the church. An antique harp stood in one lonely corner of the church, seemingly forgotten by time. Slowly the trio made their way down the candle lit aisle towards the coffin. As they drew closer William noticed, peculiarly, that the box was empty. Questioningly, he looked down to the children.

"What's the meaning of this?!" he asked, confusion evident in his rising voice. With large, sad eyes the little girl pulled free of William's hand and crawled into the coffin, followed by her brother.

Chills traveled the length of William's spine as the two children lay back in an embrace, began turning grey, and started to rot away. William's mouth hung open in horror. He spun around and was confronted by the mourners. Corpses filled the wooden benches. Skeletal faces, locked in horrible grins, mocked him. He seemed to recognize some of the dead. Sister Mary Ann and others from the convent sat with gruesome smiles on their decaying faces.

Outside, the skies were black and the whistle of wind through the cracks in the walls threatened to vanquish the flames of the candles that gave light to this funeral of the damned. Surrounded by death, William Bell started down the aisle toward the doorway. The ghoulish audience turned under strained, decaying flesh and snapping, brittle, bones to allow their dead eyes to keep him locked in their soulless gaze.

Halfway down the aisle familiar footsteps echoed through the haunted church as they ascended the steps outside the door, footsteps that he knew all too well. William placed the back of his fist to his mouth attempting to hold back his desire to scream. The familiar form of his dead father stood before him, his skeletal face half hidden by shadows, silver tipped cane in hand. His father, the abusive monster that destroyed his childhood, that hated him like no other. His father, the one that beat him, nearly to death, on one fateful occasion, stepped closer. How William had rejoiced when his father had died, but this nightmare refused to stay dead, the grave not comforting enough.

"How does it feel to live a lie, boy?" the wraith hissed, pointing at him with his cane.

"Father," William uttered, "How?"

"Tell me your tale now!" the dead man continued, ignoring William's question, "A soul from half truths, half ends, and half starts. No past...No future...Just an ever present mistake that only the grave can correct."

Isabella Beniot glided into the church, her dead feet dragging on the wood. A scream of terror escaped William as his dead lover hovered beside the animated remains of his dead father. Her empty eyes looked accusingly at him, her black hair whipping wildly about. Then all of the dead were on their feet.

William's father took Isabella by the hand as the congregation of corpses encircled him.

He spun in place, staring at the grinning faces that now surrounded him, reaching for him.

There was no escape this time. He dropped to his knees reciting prayers as dead hands fell upon him, tearing at him. The wave of death constricted, smothering him with the rotting smell of the grave. His screams were so loud that he thought his own ear drums would burst, then darkness overtook him, hurtling him back to reality.

William sat up abruptly, his scream carrying over from his hellish realm of the lost, into the material world. In the waning sunlight his screams resounded throughout the woods, sounding as if a score of the dying had come face to face with the reaper of souls himself. Looking about, bewildered, he found that he was in the middle of a lonely, earthen road. Sweat soaked his filth covered clothing. His insides twisted in violent spasms as bile rose in his throat and vomit spewed forth from his mouth purging what small amount of nourishment that he was able to force down earlier. His nose burning and throat raw, he pushed himself to his feet. Turning about on the trail way he searched for any signs of his missing mount but found none. William looked up into the dark skies as the blood red sun effortlessly descended behind the wooded horizon.

Fear and hopelessness manifested as tears rose and welled in his eyes as his gaze shifted back to the trail slowly being cover by the discarded leaves from this past autumn, whipped about by the rising winds. With this path, fading in the shadows of evening, stretching out before him, he began running. There was nothing else he could do.

Chapter 7

Brusion Beniot slowed his great horse to a trot. The distinct smell of burnt wood and scorched earth filled his nostrils. Moving off of the worn road, he followed the erratic trail that his prey had made. A smile of satisfaction spread across his chiseled face. Bell was no horseman, that was obvious. Almost as obvious as the trail that he had left. There had been no attempt to conceal his direction of travel. Soon, he would have him and vindicate the injustice that William Bell had bestowed upon his family. Soon, he would avenge his sister's death in the only way that he deemed appropriate; the suffering and death of William Bell.

But, Brusion was getting ahead of himself. First he must find the fiend. The winding trail that Bell had left tore through the woodland with brute force, almost as if he had lost control of his mount. With eagle like precision, Brusion scanned his surroundings. A small object, just ahead on the make shift trail, caught his eye. Dismounting his horse, Brusion approached what had earned his attention. He carefully examined the small, tattered, piece of fabric that was held fast by vicious thorns. He reached out and removed the swath of cloth. Sliding his hand inside of his vest, he removed the worn piece of William Bell's cloak and compared it with the ragged cloth that he had just found.

"The texture…The color… My God, even the smell!" Brusion thought. It was a match. It was Bell's, of that he had no doubt. Brusion closed his powerful fist, as if his crushing grip would somehow cause Bell pain. He peered further down the trail into what looked to be a small clearing in the heart of a valley. Reaching back, he took his horses' reins and led it onward through the thick bramble. Stepping out of the underbrush of the forest Brusion saw the smoking, charred ruins of what once was a large structure. He walked close to the smoldering framework, its once impressive tower now collapsed in ruin. Red hot embers glowed and spat angrily, refusing to succumb. Staring about this scene of carnage, Brusion spotted a robed figure standing beside what he thought to be freshly covered graves. He moved closer to the figure and could now tell for certain that this was, indeed, a burial ground, with several modest markers denoting the older graves.

"What happened here?" he called out.

The nun turned to face him, exposing her grief.

"Young man," the elderly woman began, "I have long served the Lord unquestioningly, for nearly my entire life. I have seen pain and I have seen suffering. I have witnessed despair and death. I have seen these things befall countless souls, good and Godly people, as well as those that were much deserving of God's wrath. I was always reassured by his word and in turn reassured others that all was part of God's plan, his will. Now I stand before you left to wonder, is mine a true soul or just a cruel mockery of another's beliefs?"

Tears poured down the woman's defeated face. Brusion shifted uneasily, unaware of any words of comfort that he could offer. He dropped his gaze to the heaped dirt atop the seven fresh graves, trying to make sense of the old nun's ramblings.

"What happened here, Sister?" he asked again.

"Days ago, that wretch found us. He prophesied of fiery destruction and the burning of angels!" she wailed. "We took him for a madman, but if we had headed his warnings these angels might yet live!" she sobbed, waving her trembling hand back and forth over the new graves.

Brusion now stood beside the distraught woman.

"You said, he?" he began, keeping his voice just above a whisper. "Who was he?"

The nun looked up into Brusion's eyes, her face a twisted combination of confusion, loss, and fear. She raised her burned and blistered hands towards the sky. A deranged smile spread across her smut covered face.

"Why, our messiah!" she cackled "The messiah, the messiah!" she repeated as she fell to her knees and began praying over the graves.

"We should have heeded the messiah's words!" she exclaimed.

"Madness!" Brusion spat as he stepped away from the old woman back towards his mount. He climbed onto his horse and turned back towards the wooded trail leaving the deranged old woman to her delusions. Suddenly, movement near the tree line triggered Brusion's finely honed reflexes and he swiftly drew his flintlock pistol, leveling it on the shadowy figure emerging from the woods. The figure paused, sitting down a wooden bucket, its contents sloshing over the rim. Raising her hand in a gesture of greeting, another of the surviving nuns began to approach the unknown rider.

"Sir, please!" she began, "Do us no harm, please! Enough has been done to us already."

Brusion carefully lowered his pistol and placed it back in its holster near the small of his back.

"What happened here?" he questioned, hoping for a better answer than he had received from the distraught old nun who still babbled over the graves. "All that she offered was mad ramblings of the death of angels and the coming of a messiah." he continued, motioning to the crazed old woman, whose face was now buried in the soil, sobbing.

"Forgive her, please," the nun said, her voice full of exhaustion. "Sister Frances nearly perished in the fire which claimed seven of our order. Many other were badly injured and may not survive. Our home here is gone and it is all too much for her to take. We stayed behind to bury our dead. Come morning we leave to join the others."

Brusion stared at the woman, calculating her words.

"What caused this tragedy?" he asked.

The nun's voice quivered as she told the story.

"During the hours before the fire a man that we had found in the woods warned one of our sisters of an apocalyptic vision involving fire and death. I overheard his conversation with sweet Sister Mary Ann, rest her soul. She perished in the fire. After issuing his warning he fled our home upon his mount, leaving us to our fate."

"What did this man look like?" Brusion asked, "Can you describe him to me, Sister?"

"He was slender and of average height," she spoke softly, "with long, golden hair. He wore a cloak that was torn and tattered, much like his clothing was."

Removing the piece of cloth that he had found upon the trail, Brusion held it up for the nun to inspect.

"Was this the color of his cloak?" he questioned.

"Yes." She replied, fear evident, "He seemed a truly tortured soul."

Shoving the cloth back into his vest, Brusion spoke through clinched teeth, "A tortured soul, you say? No. He is a charlatan and a murderer of innocents. He has no soul to speak of. And soon he will pay for his crimes."

Placing a hand to her lips, a horrified look befalling her, she asked, "What of the other one, the girl?"

"What girl?" He replied.

"One of our lost, swore, as death took her, that there was another stranger within our halls. A young woman moving through the corridors while the fire was raging, cutting down any that crossed her path." She said.

"Tell me, what did this girl look like?" Bruson asked.

Sister Frances rose from the graves and ran towards them.

"She had hair the color of midnight skies and a face worthy of the dead, her red dress trimmed in the gold of Heaven!" she screeched. "She brought the fires of judgement to us!"

"You saw this?" Brusion exclaimed, "With your own eyes?!"

The near hysterical old woman yelled, "I saw her! I saw her!" her shrieks startling a bird in its nest, causing it to take flight.

"I've been praying to her!" she continued, her tone growing more crazed, a combination of laughter and sobs, "She revealed herself to me! He is the messiah! The messiah of death!" she cackled. "And she, she is the scythe that harvests souls!"

The distraught old woman collapsed to the ground in a heap, the other nun dropping to her knees to tend to her.

"So, the chains of your sins lengthen, link by link, you devil." Brusion spoke, his thoughts on William Bell, "But soon your murderous ways will be brought to an end."

The young nun looked up from her attempt to comfort Sister Frances.

"You are searching for them, are you not?"

Brusion nodded slowly.

"Then go, sir," she replied, "find the ones responsible for this atrocity."

Looking back to her ruined home, then allowing her gaze to drift to her friend's fresh graves, she turned back to Brusion.

"Kill them, sir! God help me!" she said as tears streaked her dirty cheeks, "Kill them both!"

Brusion turned his horse and spurred it into the woods, back towards the road, to escape the madness that had befallen the nuns. William Bell's red dressed companion? A shiver overtook Brusion as goose flesh covered his muscular body. The old nun had described his dead sister, Isabella, perfectly, right down to the golden trim of her burial gown.

Chapter 8

It was well into the night when William Bell beheld the warm glow of candle light from quiet window sills, disrupting the blanket of darkness ahead. His breathing was a series of rasping wheezes. He pressed on, pushing his body farther than he thought humanly possible. Just as in his vision, he had run for what seemed like hours. He found himself on the outskirts of the sleepy village, overlooked in its entirety, by the old church from his nightmares, which stood high upon a hill.

He winced, the pain from his blistered feet slowing his once long strides to a pathetic, limping trot. He made his way into the small community, the muddy roads of the village sucking him down, making each step an effort. Wagon trails stood out among the footprints on the muddied path. He stood, now, at the very place from his nightmare. The church from his dream loomed high on a hill in the distance, its steeple silhouetted against the sky overlooking the village.

"What can I do to prevent this appalling vision from coming to pass?" he wondered. He knew he had to find a way. The eerie silence of the slumbering village streets was ended by the distant trot of a horse approaching. William looked about, trying to discern the origin of the sound. Materializing out of the darkness, a rider appeared from around the side of a small wooden cottage.

There was a long silence as the rider stared at William Bell.

"What business do you have here stranger?" the horseman asked in an authoritative tone, "And at this godless hour?"

"Who...Who are you, sir?" William stammered.

"My name is Sheriff Nathaniel Winston, Sir," the man replied, moving his heavy coat to the side, exposing his badge which was barely visible in the candle light, "and I'll have you know that vagabonds are not welcome here. You would do well to state your business, and if you have none here, then you will remove yourself from this village immediately."

"Sir," William began, desperation apparent in his voice, "I am here to prevent a terrible travesty from happening and I am in need of your assistance!"

The barrel chested Sheriff looked down at William Bell, his eyes squinting and his hand resting on the pistol at his waist.

"Go on." he replied, "I'm listening."

"Sir," William Bell responded, "There is no time to waste! We have to get to the children!"

"What?" the Sheriff asked as he dismounted his horse, "What children? What are you talking about?"

"Please!" William pleaded, "These children will die!"

"Alright," Sheriff Winston said approaching William Bell, "You will come with me. Now."

William looked about for a route of escape, wondering if his tired legs could outrun the middle aged man. Upon seeing this, the Sheriff drew his pistol, aiming it at William Bell's chest and repeated, "You will come with me. Now."

William walked through the muddy streets past several shops, following spoken commands. His armed captor remained a few steps behind, leading his horse. William was ordered to stop before a small, two story complex on what must have been the main street of this small community.

"Don't move, now, lad." the sheriff commanded, as he tied his horse to a post in front of the structure, never removing William Bell from his watchful eye. The sheriff then circled around to William and motioned towards the building with his pistol.

William stepped upon the creaking wooden porch that extended in front of the building, ushered by Sheriff Winston.

"Inside" Winston commanded, turning his head, eyes shifting side to side, to assure they weren't being followed. William turned the doorknob and stepped into the jail. The insides were crude and unpainted. In no way was this place comforting or welcoming. Against the far wall of the room bars from floor to ceiling formed a cell. William's heart sank as he realized his predicament.

"Into the cell" The man said, his pistol still trained on William's torso.

"Why," Bell protested, "I've done nothing! Do you not understand? I'm trying to keep this village's children safe!"

"So am I!" spat the Sheriff as he shoved William Bell into the cell.

The Sheriff slammed the cell door shut with a loud metallic thud. He quickly locked the door as

William Bell approached the bars, pleading, "Please, sir!"

"You will shut your mouth if you know what's good for you." barked the Sheriff, causing William to cease his outcry.

He walked over to a shoddy table in the room, removed his brimmed hat and placed it upon a hook protruding from the plank wall. Several large rings with attached keys adorned similar hooks on the wall. The ruddy faced man placed his pistol upon the table and ran a leather gloved hand through his dark, curly hair as he turned back to William Bell. He motioned to a small wooded stool inside of William's cell. William took a deep breath and had a seat upon the stool, thankful to rest his tired body even in this jail cell.

The Sheriff pulled off his gloves and shoved them into his coat pockets as he seated himself on the corner of the old wooden table before the cell. Letting his fingers stroke his curled mustache, the Sheriff eyed William suspiciously. He took a deep breath and spoke.

"What is your name?"

"William." He replied. "William Bell."

"So, Mister Bell, tell me about these children."

William tried to collect himself, unsure of how to explain his claims. Sweat rose on his brow. He couldn't tell if his returning fever was the cause or his frayed nerves. Wiping the sweat from his eyes with his dirt covered hand, William Bell prepared to tell his strange tale. The sound of a man's heavy footfall, crossing the outside porch with haste, stopped William before he spoke. A harsh knock sounded at the door followed by a gruff voice yelling, "Sheriff! Sheriff!"

Standing up, the Sheriff approached the door.

"Yes?" he asked loudly, "What is the matter, man?!"

The door swung open and a hefty man in heavily worn clothing covered in mud, stepped into the jail. With a look of urgency on his face, he once again stammered, "Sheriff! You are needed at the Taylor farm!"

"It is late, Thomas, and I am busy." the Sheriff stated, motioning to the stranger in the cell, "Can it not wait until morning?"

"Sheriff," the distraught man continued, "They have been brutalized! Murdered!"

The Sheriff grabbed his hat from the hook, looking wide eyed at the man.

"Who, man?" he asked, "Who has been murdered?"

Before he could answer the Sheriff, William Bell answered for him.

"The children."

The Sheriff looked to William Bell then back to the villager who stood there, nodding his head in disbelief.

"Yes," he said, "He's right, the children. The girl has been drowned and the poor boy was slaughtered like a hog! The old woman Taylor was attacked, but still lives!"

William stood up and crossed the cell to stand, trembling, at the door, his hands gripping the bars until his knuckles were white. "I tried to warn you! I tried!" he said.

Sheriff Winston shifted his eyes towards the cell and grabbed his pistol from the table top.

"Watch him, carefully, man!" he commanded, motioning towards Bell as he rushed out into the street.

He hurriedly untied his horse, mounted it, and galloped off into the night towards the Taylor farm and the awaiting horror that had been described to him. Inside the jail the man in the muddied clothes sat down a good distance from the cell, nervously staring with wide eyes, at the prisoner.

William let his head fall against the bars in despair.

"I have failed." He said in a hushed voice, "Again."

The man in the room, Thomas, hung on Bell's every word.

"How many more must die to punish me," William continued, "Is life without you not hell enough?"

As if to answer there came a sound from the back of his cell, something bumping the wall from outside. William looked up to his guard, whose face had drained of all color, and appeared to be ready to bolt from the jail at any moment. The sound of finger nails scrapping down the wooded walls replaced the muffled pounding. Hair on the back of William's neck stood on end as he spun around to face the sound. Near the top of his cell was a small, shuttered opening. Cautiously, he crossed his cell, taking a moment to gather his nerves.

What was on the other side of those shutters, he wondered. *The dead, again? Come to pay another visit, tearing at the wall outside?* Was he awake now? Or caught up in another hellish vision?

He reached out a shaking hand and threw back the shutters exposing iron bars and two piercing, yellow eyes. William yelled, startled by the sight, which frightened the large owl perched on the window sill. The owl screeched as it took flight leaving the mouse, its intended prey, to the stray cat stalking the alley way outside the jail.

William took a deep breath as did his watchman. It would have been comical had the whole situation not been so dire. Overcome by exhaustion and guilt he collapsed upon the straw pile. Rolling to his side he pulled his knees up to his chest. Tears rose and streamed across his face, leaving trails of clean flesh as they washed away filth and grime.

If only these tears could wash away my sins with the same effect, He thought to himself as he wiped his face with the back of his hand. He closed his eyes and immediately drifted off to sleep, a distant roaring in his ears and the far away sound of, what seemed to him, to be a beautifully played harp ushering him away.

Chapter 9

Sheriff Winston pushed his horse on, faster. His mind on dead children and the strange man locked away in his jail. At first he assumed that this William Bell was just a drunkard that had found his way into the little village, but his gut instinct immediately told him that this was not the case. There was something sinister about this young man, something not quite right and the sheriff was glad that he had went with his gut feeling and took him into custody. This stranger arrives and now children are dead. He prayed that this was not the case, that the children were alive, that this was just a terrible misunderstanding.

He could see torch light up ahead. A group of the villagers were standing together no doubt awaiting his arrival. There was a solemnness about the gathering, near the gently bubbling brook that ran along the edge of the Taylor farm, trailing off into the woods. The sheriff's horse trotted to a stop and he quickly dismounted. The torchlight exposed familiar faces, horror stricken and long with sorrow.

"They are over there." One of the villagers spoke, his voice cracking as he extended a trembling arm and pointed towards an old broken down wagon which was missing part of one of its wheels. Sheriff Winston pushed through the group of distraught towns people and rushed to the old wagon. His heart pounded in his throat as he neared the small dark forms lying still beneath the cart. Dropping to his knees and peering under it he could make out bodies but the shadows concealed the identities. The Sheriff looked back to the crowd.

"I need light, here!" he yelled, mounting desperation creeping into his voice. "Bring me a torch!"

One of the villagers, startled out of mourning, moved forward and made his way to the kneeling sheriff. Sheriff Winston reached up and took the torch and the man slinked back away from the scene, refusing to look upon it. Nathaniel Winston turned back to the wagon and clinched his jaws as he illuminated the ghastly secrets that the shadows held. There in the wet grass, beneath the wagon, lay the children of the widower; Landon Taylor. The morbid expression on the brother and sister's faces betrayed the events that took their lives. The boy's face was bloody and bruised, the tint of his flesh already greying. His body was blood soaked, savaged by numerous long deep cuts. The boy's sister, however, showed no signs of violence save for the deep purple bruise around her throat, which told the story of her demise. He reached out and gently moved the little girl's hair from her face. Her eyes stared at him blankly, mouth open wide as if a scream that would never come was trying to escape her bluish lips. The sheriff blinked back tears of anger and sorrow as he examined the bodies. He noticed a tuff of raven black hair clinched tightly in the dead girl's tiny fist. Sheriff Winston opened her hand and took the lock of hair. Holding it close, he could smell the odor of decay.

"These children's clothing are wet." Sheriff Winston called back to the group, some of whom had moved in closer to him. "Has anyone checked the brook and the woods beyond?"

"No, sheriff." One of the men replied, swallowing hard.

"Sheriff, the children's grandmother witnessed the attack!" another man said.

"Where is she?!" the sheriff questioned, his anger barely suppressed.

"She is inside being comforted by neighbors." The man answered.

Sheriff Winston gathered his composure as he barked orders, "Take a group of men and search the area around the bed of the brook, search the woods as well. Keep your guard up, men. There is a killer among us."

As the group of men headed off the sheriff turned to face the small wooden house across the field, the one with dim candle light being cast from its windows, through cracked shutters, the one with horrible wailing coming from inside. Pulling his hat down tight he walked away from the dead children towards the house, the tuff of black hair clinched in his gloved fist.

"Where is Landon Taylor, the children's father?" the sheriff asked one of the villagers that followed him.

"The old woman said that he left by wagon two days ago, heading north to gather supplies for the coming planting season." He answered.

"How horrible that this will be his homecoming." Sheriff Winston replied, "We had best send someone for him."

"I will see to it, myself." said the man as Sheriff Winston handed him the torch. He quickly turned and left to make preparations for his journey.

Standing outside the entrance of the small farmhouse the sheriff listened to the sorrowful cries coming from within. He tried to gather his thoughts and words but what do you say to someone facing a loss such as this? He glanced around, his mind a jumble of emotions. In the dim candle light radiating from the sconce beside the door, he spotted a small wooden chair, too small, even, for the children. A tiny crude doll, tattered from years of play, sat in the chair, its black eyes staring, blankly out into the night. The little girl's toy, no doubt, found waiting for a playmate that would never return. Gritting his teeth, the muscles in his neck tensing with heartbreaking anger, the sheriff pushed the door open and stepped inside.

The sorrow of death was heavy in the small room, heavy like a physical thing. In one corner sat an old woman, her face resting in her hands. Heaving cries of anguish came from her shaking body. Two of the village women sat at her side, attempting to console her. The sound of the sheriff closing the door caused the old woman to raise her head. She peered through swollen, red eyes at Nathaniel Winston.

"Sheriff!" the old woman began, her voice breaking and whole body trembling, "Nathaniel, she murdered my babies."

The sheriff's eyes widened. *She?* he thought. He had expected to hear that the murderer was a man, the very man that was locked away at his jail! In fact, the one who had warned of this tragic event. His eyes dropped, not wanting to hold the old woman's gaze, not wanting to stare into that vast void of pain.

"You saw her?" the sheriff asked, forcing himself to look at the grieving woman, "A woman did this?"

"Oh, yes! I saw her!" She exclaimed, "The witch sprang forth from the woods like some wild beast. She set upon Samantha as she was returning from fetching water from the brook, grabbing her by her throat. She dragged her into the water. The poor child tried to fight, to get away, but she couldn't break the monster's grip! The devil then dealt a stunning blow to the back of her head and held her below the water's surface. Her brother, Fritz, ran into the water to his sister's aid, however the woman easily, almost effortlessly, tossed him to the side and produced a harvest sickle from the folds of her dress. She then attacked the boy with a beast like fury, the blade cut into his body, his blood spilling into the creek. He pulled himself from the water and attempted to flee as she slashed at his back. He tried to crawl under the wagon to escape her, his pitiful screams for mercy ignored, as she followed, hacking at him with her curved blade. I myself, ran towards the scene, but this old body lacked the speed or strength to aid them. The devil stopped only long enough to glare up from my poor grandson with blood, not her own, covering her horrible face. She looked at me, her expression that of an enraged animal. It was nearly dark and though most of her face was held by shadows, her movements and cursing voice betrayed her mask of darkness. It was that horrid woman who dropped my Fritz, bloody and broken, and pulled herself from beneath the wagon. She crossed the field towards me, arms extended and shrieking, where I stood frozen with fear. Her fine red dress flowed upon the breeze, its golden trim, shimmering in the light of the rising moon. Then I was in her grasp. Her long black hair hung, matted about her face. Her soulless eyes glared into mine. Her hands held me in a painful grip, one which I took to be my end. I could smell roses and the stench of decaying flesh as she paused, eyeing me with ghoulish amusement."

"Well, old woman?" she spoke to me in a voice worthy of the mad, "Do you speak your pain? Challenge me? You stand before the fruits of hell."

"I could do nothing before her, speak, scream, nor run. I could only stare into the shadows, looking at the sagging, rotting face of this monster. In the distance, the sound of an approaching horse caught the fiend's attention and she turned her head to peer towards the road. I, too, could hear the horse approach. With all of the strength that I could gather in these old lungs, I screamed as loud as I could, hoping that the rider would hear me. Alas, a saddled horse with no rider trotted up the path, looking near starved. It snorted and stopped to drink in the bloody waters of the brook."

"My steed thirsts for blood as well." She cackled. The witch turned back to me with a demonic smile spreading across her face.

"Speak your pain quietly, old one," she growled at me, "for the end may scream back!"

Then my world went black. When I awoke, the beast was gone. The moon was high and I could see my sweet babies by its light. Samantha, face down in the water, caught in the bend of the brook and Fritz, lying, dead, beneath the wagon, where the monster had finished him. I screamed and screamed, too afraid to move. Thankfully Thomas heard me and came to my aid. Why spare an old woman, such as me, and end lives so young, so innocent? I don't understand, Nathanial."

The old woman slowly rose to her feet, the two women at her side also rising, arms posed, unsure what to do. She unsteadily crossed the room and grabbed the sheriff's hand.

"Nathaniel," she sobbed, "What am I to do? My son left his children in my charge and I have let them both die! His wife, Abagail, the children's mother, has been in the grave but a year and now the children join her! This cannot have happened! This is a horrible dream! Please, someone," she begged looking to the faces in the room, "please wake me up!"

Nathaniel placed his arms around the old woman. Blinking back tears, he found himself at a loss of what to say. There was no comforting her. After a long moment of silence, he spoke with a quivering voice, "I will find this culprit...These children will have justice. I promise that these crimes will be paid for."

The sheriff's thoughts raced back to the stranger locked up in his jail and the eerie prophecy that he had delivered.

"Stay here, with her," he told the women as he eased the distraught old woman back to her chair. "I will appoint some of the men to stand guard outside until my return. I will not be long."

The women nodded as their attention shifted back to the poor woman. The sheriff turned and left the farmhouse, issuing a few brief commands to some of the villagers, as he mounted his horse and headed back to the jail, back to the stranger and whatever answers he held.

Chapter 10

The sound of the mechanism clanking inside of the iron lock as it opened jarred William Bell from his restless sleep. Rolling over to face the cell bars, William struggled to wake his body, which seemed disconnected from his brain and nerves, refusing even the most simple of requests. After long moments he finally took control of himself, sitting up in the pile of straw, dust from his nest filling his nose.

Standing before him was the large form of Sheriff Winston, his dark eyes peering accusingly. In his right hand, the sheriff clutched the wooden handle of his flint lock pistol, which he held at the ready by his side. The hefty man, Thomas, who had served as jailer slowly and cautiously slipped into the cell, through the open door and made his way over to William. In his hands he carried a set of iron shackles. William Bell looked from the man to the sheriff.

"They were dead? The children?" he muttered with despair in his voice.

"Yes." the sheriff replied, his voice empty of all emotion.

"Extend your wrists." The lawman ordered ,"These restraints are for your safety as well as ours while we get this sorted out."

Hesitantly, William Bell held out his arms to the man holding the shackles. Thomas, nervously, fidgeted with the cuff locks until they were tight and securely locked around William's wrists. He was led out of the jail and into the street, where he was assisted in mounting a waiting horse. The Sheriff and the villager then climbed into the saddles of their own horses. The trio of men rode slowly through the empty streets, heading to the long solitary path that led to the Taylor farm.

At this point the sheriff's companion broke the monotony of the ride.

"Is he the one, Nathaniel?" he whispered, "Did he do it?"

"What were you doing, out this far away from your home? And so late?" the sheriff asked Thomas, ignoring his question.

"Sheriff!" he began defensively, mouth dropped open and eyes wide, "Are you insinuating that I had something to do with this?"

"Of course not, Thomas. I'm just trying to put all of the pieces together."

"Oh.... Alright, then." Thomas replied, relaxing a bit, "I had visited with my brother. We had drank a bit too much ale and I had fallen asleep. When I woke I decided to go home. On my way I thought that I heard a scream coming from the Taylor farm. I had spoken to Landon a few days ago and knowing that he was away I merely went to check on his mother and the children." His head dropped slightly as he spoke, "If only I had been a few moments earlier perhaps those poor children would still live."

William Bell kept silent but listened attentively.

"There was no way that you could have helped. No one could have. Those children have been dead for hours." Sheriff Winston said as he brought his gaze to rest, unsettlingly, on Bell.

"What did you find when you arrived at the farm?" he asked Thomas.

"Well," Thomas spoke, pondering deeply so as not to leave out any detail, "I was right about here." he said, looking at his surroundings, attempting to pin point his earlier location, "heading home, when I thought I heard a scream. I paused here for a moment and listened and again I heard what I knew to be a woman's shriek. I spurred my old horse on as hard as I could, down the path towards the farm. When I rode into the clearing overlooking the Taylor's homestead, I saw old lady Taylor, sprawled in the field. I rode across to her and dismounted. Her face was pale as death! I thought that she was surely a corpse but as I stood over her she began to stir and mumble, "The children, the children!" Then she sat upright and released a horrible shriek.

"The children!" she yelled again!

I turned and looked in the direction that she was pointing; toward the brook. I saw the girl, face down in the water near the bank. I ran to her as fast as I could but, it was too late. She was already dead. I gathered her up and carried her from the water. That is when I noticed the boy, his body badly mutilated, lying beneath the wagon. His death was not an easy one, Nathanial. He suffered tremendously. I placed the girl's body beneath the wagon where her brother lay. Other neighbors had heard the screams and came to investigate. They began caring for the old woman and I mounted up and came straight to you."

The testimony ended as the three men now halted their mounts at the edge of the Taylor property. William Bell sat, horrified, by the story that he had just heard. Several figures with torches, stood watch near the old wagon, under which the slain children lay. Villagers with torches darted in and out of sight among the trees and bushes that lined the brook, blinking in the dark like giant fireflies, as they covered the grounds, searching for an unseen killer. As the three men rode across the open field the villagers turned and stared, questioningly, at the shackled stranger. The once small group of people had swelled as news of the murders spread through the farming community. Some of the onlookers were there to offer comfort in this time of hardship, others were there to see for themselves what their hearts refused to let their minds believe. Already stories of a supernatural creature lurking in the woods were spreading through the growing crowd.

A murmur of questions erupted from within the group as they watched the men approach the farm house. Suggestions as to who the stranger was, speculations as to what he had done to belong in custody, quickly drawn conclusions, all washed through the gathering towns people. Keeping their distance, the group slowly followed the sheriff and his companions. The sheriff stopped his horse near the front of the cottage, swung his leg over, and quickly dropped to the ground. He looked briefly up at William Bell and then to the growing crowd, numbering at least twenty by his count. Many carried torches, setting the country side awash with light.

Sheriff Winston knew that he must conduct this quickly as these people needed a focal point for their outrage. Although he knew them all and they were mostly godly people, in this state of high emotion a stranger in chains could fast become a victim in a noose should the mob decide that he was, in some way, responsible. For now, William Bell was innocent. The sheriff stepped to the door and rapped lightly as he pushed it open and walked inside.

William looked about nervously, fidgeting in the saddle, his gaze shifting from Thomas, who was eyeing him quietly and suspiciously, to the mob behind them. It seemed more torches were approaching from the tree line in the distance. William wondered to himself if this was how a fox feels during a hunt? When the unrelenting hounds would overtake him?

The faces, illuminated by torch light, stared back at him with mixed emotions: fear, disgust, outrage, despair, and some beamed with relief. William realized that he must look guilty to the people, a stranger in shackles at the scene of a murder and in company of the sheriff. William Bell himself would have made the same assumptions that some of the crowd had made, that the killer was captured. How unfortunate, he thought, they were wrong. The killer was out there now, probably watching and enjoying this scene of carnage that was so masterfully crafted.

The cottage door opened once more. Outlined by the gentle candle light from within, stood Sheriff Winston, with his helping arm around the bent form of the old lady Taylor. Together, they stepped out into the night. The old woman tried, in vain, to hold back her tears from the crowd of onlookers. Sheriff Winston reached and took the torch from Thomas, who still sat upon his horse. Turning back to the old woman the sheriff tried to reassure her.

"Try to be strong," he whispered, "for the children."

The old woman nodded and the sheriff extended the torch toward the stranger mounted beside Thomas, casting light upon him for her to see his face.

"Have you seen this man before?" the sheriff asked, his voice loud and authoritative. A long silence befell the gathering as the old woman silently studied the stranger before her. The wind blew gently and William's hair, free from the ribbon that usually kept it back, spilled about his face. William looked into the elderly woman's eyes, pitying the torture that she was feeling. The old woman's mouth hung open at first, her lips trembling. With a quite voice, filled with heartbreak, she answered, "No."

The crowd erupted in whispers as the villagers began conversing about the stranger and the nights events. William Bell breathed a sigh of relief in hopes that he would soon be free, free to leave this village and take with him the curse that he brought. Sheriff Winston looked up to William Bell, unsure what to make of a man who predicts death. There was much to discuss with this stranger before he could be released and if he was not guilty, then a killer was still among them.

"Sheriff Winston! Sheriff Winston!" a voice called from the distance. "We found a horse!"

The sheriff, as well as the crowd, turned to see several men with torches leading an old nag out of the woods. The chatter of the crowd continued as the men approached with the animal. Sheriff Winston stood beside old lady Taylor, his arm, still, about her shoulders. The crowd of villagers separated, allowing the men leading the horse to pass between them. As the group stepped before the sheriff and the grieving woman, William Bell spoke for the first time in front of the crowd.

"Sheriff, that is my poor horse." He said.

"Oh, Nathanial!" the old woman shrieked, her hand covering her mouth, "That is her steed, the starving horse that drinks the blood of children!"

Sheriff Winston looked from the mounted stranger in shackles to the sobbing old woman. Relinquishing his grip from around the old woman's shoulders, he walked over to the horse, its ribs visible in the torchlight. The animal snorted nervously, as the sheriff opened the pommel bag to investigate its contents. A hush came over the crowd as the Sheriff rifled through William Bell's meager belongings.

"And this is your horse?" The sheriff turned and asked William, "You are sure of it?"

"Yes, sir" He replied in a quite voice.

William Bell's blood seemed to freeze in his veins as the sheriff withdrew a blood covered sickle from within the pouch.

A growl of rage escaped the old woman as she lunged forward towards William Bell, slapping and clawing. Her terrible shrieks and the fury of her assault caught the shackled man and horse that he was mounted on by surprise. The animal shifted quickly and William Bell toppled from the saddle. The old woman was upon him, her nails digging into his face.

"They were babies!" she screeched again and again. The sheriff rushed forward, grabbing the elderly woman and separated her from the stunned and helpless man.

"Take her into the house!" he ordered the bystanders, as he turned back to William Bell.

"She killed my grandson with that blade and he is in league with her!" the old woman yelled to the crowd, "She killed my Fritz with that blade!"

The hysterical woman collapsed, sobbing at the doorway of the farmhouse. Several of the men rushed forward and helped her to her feet, assisting her into her home. The sheriff wasted no time in grabbing William Bell in his strong hands. He hefted the shackled man up with great force. The old woman's convictions echoed through the mob of villagers as the enraged community began shouting demands for vengeance. The sheriff pushed Bell towards the horse that had thrown him.

"Mount up, quickly!" he said as the angry crowd began closing in.

William pulled himself upon the horse as Sheriff Winston grabbed its reins.

The sheriff looked at William.

"A woman may have murdered the children but you come here with the knowledge of the crimes, and the murder's weapon amongst your belongings on your horse? You know much more than what you have admitted. Part of me longs to give you to them." The sheriff said, looking about at the increasingly hostile mob, "but you will have a chance to tell me your secrets and, at the very least, the children's father deserves to see those responsible for their deaths hanged. Hold tight and do not fall, for if you do there may well be another death on this farm tonight."

With a terrified protest William spoke, "But sheriff, I have done nothing but try to help!"

The sheriff spurred on his horse, followed by William Bell and Thomas.

"With this being the product of your help," Thomas yelled, "I suspect that your reward may well be the gallows!"

"Dear God, help me!" William Bell prayed as they rode, looking to the distant church on the hill, visible in the moon light over the tree tops. It must have been the residuum of the vision in his troubled mind, but he thought, for an instant that he saw a figure in red standing in one of the upper windows of the church.

The three galloped across the field away from the angry mob and the horrors of the farm, and towards the trail leading back to the small town, towards the safety of the jail.

William Bell was once more racing for his survival with failure resulting in death and once more the sound was with him, laughing at him, taunting him... slowly killing him.

Chapter 11

William paced the floor of his familiar cell, his boot heel echoing his steps loudly in the wooden building. The sounds of the angry mob outside penetrated the jail walls, screaming for attention, screaming for justice, screaming for his death. It was always worse at night. For nearly a week William had sat incarcerated within this cell, listening as the volume of the crowd grew, as more and more outraged townspeople gathered, only dispersing in the early hours of morning. The community would then go about its normal daily activities while minds lingered on the accused, safe in the jail and the penance that had yet to be paid. Like the tide coming in, as anger built throughout the day, it was released nightly. This night had been worse. Sheriff Winston stood outside the cell bars looking in at the imprisoned man. William looked at the sheriff, who was watching his every move. Rushing forward to the bars, William Bell exploded with despair.

"Please," he pleaded, "I have done nothing wrong!"

The sheriff stood unflinching.

"We have scoured the entire area, the woods, the farms, everywhere, and no one, save old woman Taylor, has seen your lady companion, the one whom was witnessed killing the children. We have your horse and the murder's weapon was found upon it yet you refuse to tell us who or where she is. If you were to give her up perhaps we could believe that you were indeed trying to help. But as it stands you are protecting a murderer of children and that makes you just as guilty as the one who took their lives. Unless you decide to confess what you know, when the father of those children arrives home, you will pay for her crimes with your life."

Sheriff Winston let an amused smile play across his face as the roar of the mob outside grew louder.

"How strange it is. This cell that you so desperately seek to be free of is the only thing that is keeping you alive. If you were to step outside of this jail the people of this town would tear you to pieces and I would be powerless to stop them. In truth? I am not sure that I would stop them. Two children rest in the church in their coffins tonight, awaiting burial and here you sit, safe and warm."

Overcome with rage, the sheriff reached through the bars and grabbed William, pulling him harshly against the cell door. William's head slammed against the bars as the Sheriff yelled, "Who is she? Where is she?"

William pushed out of the sheriff's grip and collapsed on the pile of straw in his cell, his hand dabbing at the small trickle of blood from the fresh cut near his hairline.

With his head in his hands he spoke.

"You would not believe my words if I told you."

"I don't believe you as it is." The sheriff responded, non suppressed anger apparent in his voice.

"The old woman claimed the attacks were by a devilish monster in human guise." William began, "I think she is telling the truth. You see, sheriff, I have ridden for many long months on countless roads, haunted by a young woman whom I have loved like no other before. She stays just beyond reach, just out of sight. Sometimes I swear that I can hear her voice, that I can smell her rose petal perfume. She has hair the color of raven and skin the color of snow. In My dreams she wears a long red dress trimmed with golden threads. Her name is Isabella Beniot. And she is dead."

William Bell winced as the enraged sheriff threw a chair against the cell door, startling him.

"You lie!" he bellowed, "Two children rot in the boxes and you make a mockery of it!"

Reaching into his pocket, the sheriff withdrew the tuff of black hair that he had recovered from the dead girl's grip.

"This was in the dead child's hand, ripped from her attacker's head!" he proclaimed, extending his evidence into William's cell. "It was no ghost that committed these murders. It was flesh and blood!"

Taking a deep breath, the sheriff tried to compose himself. William looked on, his heart breaking at the sight of the lock of hair in the sheriff's grip.

"I will find this 'Isabella Beniot', Mr. Bell, and I will hang you both." Nathaniel Winston promised. The sheriff turned and left the room leaving William Bell to the silence of his ghosts.

Chapter 12

William sat in the corner of his cell, his thoughts brutalizing his psyche.

"This damned waiting," he contemplated to himself, "this is perhaps worse than the end that awaits me!"

He flinched as he poured some of his drinking water over the open wounds of his blistered feet in a painful effort to cleanse them. The cool water flooded the hideous holes in his flesh with the sensation of fire. William felt as if he were losing his grip on reality all together. After her death, Isabella haunted his dreams, but now it seems she had crossed that bridge from nightmares to reality. How could this be? Was he mad? Was his lover really stalking him from the grave? Did she claw her way out of the earth to torture him with visions? Showing him innocents that were destined to die by her hand but leaving him powerless to stop her murderous rampages? Powerless, just as he was, to stop her death.

Was he truly what the people of this village thought he was? A raving maniac? A mad dog that deserved to be put down, ending the chance of him brining harm to anyone ever again?

A soft voice shook William from his thoughts of despair and self-pity.

"Isabella?" he muttered.

The voice was muffled, coming from the next room. He struggled to make out the words. The sheriff's voice, he could hear him also. Then heavy footsteps approached the doorway. The door swung open and the sheriff strode into the room carrying a tin cup filled with water and a chunk of bread. He walked up to the cell and tossed the bread through the bars. The cup of water, he set just outside the bars, but within reach of the prisoner. The accused and the accuser stared at each other. No words passed between them. William looked away from the cold gaze that seemed to tear through his very soul. The figure in the doorway behind the sheriff caught his attention.

"Isabella?" he mumbled again.

No, this was not his Isabella. This was a pretty young woman with curly brown hair which hung to her shoulders.

"Father?" she called from the doorway

The sheriff's stone-like face came to life, his eyes widening.

"Father, I have…"

Before she could finish her sentence, Sheriff Winston turned yelling, "Out! Out of here now!"

The young woman jumped involuntarily, as did William Bell, at the authoritative outburst. Her mouth fell open in surprise and she turned like a scolded child, retreating from the room followed by the sheriff, who slammed the wooden door behind him with such force that it was nearly torn from the hinges. The force was enough that it didn't shut but bounced back, remaining slightly cracked open, allowing William to hear their conversation clearly.

"Daughter," he chastised her, "I told you to stay in this room away from the prisoner!"

"But, father," she replied, "what danger was I in? He is locked away securely in his cell."

"Do not be so naïve, daughter," Sheriff Winston said, "Have men not escaped their captors before?"

"Well?!" he asked, his voice raising.

"Yes, father." She answered meekly, embarrassed at this lecture.

"You have not heard the stories that this lunatic has spewed. You don't know what he is capable of." the sheriff continued. "We have two dead children here already, I don't want to chance adding you to their number."

The girl approached her father, who had always fell victim to her childlike charm.

"Why father," she said, "I have no fear because you would stop him."

She leaned forward and stood on the tips of her toes to kiss her father on his cheek.

"I am innocent, I tell you!" William Bell yelled from his cell, "I have harmed no one! I am innocent!"

The sheriff's daughter looked towards the cracked door that led to the cell.

"Go home, Miranda." Sheriff Winston said to his daughter as he crossed the room and pulled the door shut, muffling his prisoner's pleas, "Go home and practice your harp playing for church this Sunday. I shall be along as soon as Thomas arrives to relieve my watch."

Miranda Winston nodded to her father as she passed between two of the deputized villagers that stood guard at the jail's entrance.

"Be careful on your way home," he called after her as she stepped through the door and out into the village street, "There is still a killer on the loose." but she was already vanishing down one of the side alleys in the fading afternoon sunlight.

The sheriff turned and walked into the room where William Bell waited in his cell. Stepping over to the table, he leaned forward and blew, extinguishing one of two candles that were illuminating the area. Picking up the other candle, he moved towards the door that led from this room. Sheriff Winston looked back to William Bell, who stood hidden in the dark corner of his cell.

"If you speak to my child again," he said, the seriousness of his voice unrelenting, "I will tear out your heart with my own hands."

His warning delivered, the sheriff stepped through the portal, closing the door securely behind him, leaving William alone in the darkness.

William stood, staring into the nothing, for how long? He did not know. Time had slipped from him again. He knelt and felt blindly about his cell in search of his nightly meal. Upon finding it he sat back in the straw biting into the stale, tasteless bread. He shivered in the cold, the night chill creeping into the jail, an unwanted and unwelcome visitor. There was a low roaring in his head as the sound began its creeping advance, however, just over this sound he could hear a melody drifting into his confined area, the sound of a beautifully played harp. He couldn't help but compare it to the angelic choir from his doomed vision from weeks ago. Soon, perhaps, he would hear those angelic voices again. But, this time, he would not awake from them. This time he would be dead. Dead like Isabella.

Somewhere in his mind he could feel the sound pulsating, growing louder, and the presence was there again, whispering in the so familiar, yet unidentifiable voice.

"You sit alone," it hissed, "in a dark corner of your world, trying to build an illusion worth you surviving for. It is hopeless."

Then the sound was gone. And so was William Bell, lost to the oblivion of sleep, carried away by the beautiful sound.

Chapter 13

Early morning found William Bell wide awake. He stood in the chilly morning air, the shutters of his small window open wide, watching the sun's first light creep over the horizon. He had been awakened hours ago by one of his guards taunting him.

"The father of those murdered children should be arriving home today and then we shall see just what type of monster you really are, when you are the helpless one." The guard had said.

William had endured these accusations for a week now and all of his claims of innocence had, so far, fallen on deaf ears. In truth, he couldn't blame them. How this must look from the villager's eyes, a stranger with visions of death claiming to be stalked by his dead lover? He, too, would find it impossible to believe had the tables been turned, but it was true, all of it.

William stood at the window, now bathed in the first rays of a glorious sunrise. Tears welled in his eyes as he wondered, gravely, if this could be his last day? Motion from the corner of his vision drew his attention away from the morning beauty. A shadowy figure made her way down the alley way, outside of the jail. It was a woman, heavily layered in clothing to fight off the cold, and carrying a bundle of something in her arms. She hummed a familiar melody as she moved swiftly and carelessly along the alleyway.

"That tune that you hummed," William spoke down to the bundled woman, "I heard it last night, played upon a harp."

The surprised woman gasped and dropped her package, the cloth covering falling back to expose the contents of freshly baked bread and dried meat. Her expression of shock and fear quickly gave way to the now familiar angry features of her father, Sheriff Winston. Eyes narrowed and jaw clinched tight, she stooped and hastily gathered her dropped items.

"I apologize, madam," William spoke down to Miranda Winston, "I did not mean to frighten you."

Glaring up at him through the bars, she stood and straightened her clothing.

"What did you mean to do then?" she asked, "Because all you accomplished was getting my father's, the guard's, and your morning meal thrown into the street!"

"I apologize again," he spoke sincerely, "though I fear that this will be the last morning that I trouble anyone. The song you were humming? It was you playing on the harp last evening? I overheard your father, I mean the sheriff, telling you to go home to practice."

"Yes, it was me." Miranda replied, her cheeks still flush with anger.

"Thank you, it was lovely. It soothed me and helped me to forget her…at least for a bit." he said.

Miranda stared at the troubled face peering out from behind the bars.

"And why should you get to be soothed?" she asked "Why should you get to forget, after what you have done?"

"And what have I done?" William asked the young woman, preparing to defend himself one last time.

"You know well what you have done." The sheriff's daughter answered.

"Yes." William responded, "I suppose I do. I came here to this godless place to save those children's lives only to find that I was too late. Now I have become a sacrifice to satisfy a mourning village's desire for retribution. My death will not bring those children back and it will not bring justice."

"You have the nerve to call my home godless?" Miranda asked, appalled at his accusation.

"Is that not what it is?" William asked, "With these atrocities befalling your village, befalling me? I can find no presence of God here with my dead lover haunting these woods, killing children. She watches my agony with her dead eyes, angry that I live. She takes joy in my pain, punishing me, pushing me to end my life and join her. Perhaps with my death the scales will be balanced and she will rest, but I fear her embrace. I fear her cold lips on mine. I fear what she will do to my soul."

William stopped talking and forced a pseudo smile. Miranda eyed him cautiously.

"My father was right. You are mad. Do you truly expect me to believe the story that you just told me?" she asked.

"What story do you believe?" William questioned.

This caught the sheriff's daughter off guard.

"Well," she started, "I do believe that there was a woman on the farm, lady Taylor confirmed as much, and I do believe that she killed the children, but I also think that you had a hand in it as well. Your horse was there, again old lady Taylor said as much, and the farming tool used to kill the boy was found in your bag. How else would it have gotten there if you were not companions with the killer?"

William spoke, "I had been running from her for months. I was terribly weak from lack of food having run out of provisions many days prior to my arrival here. I passed out on the trail, some miles from your village, and tumbled from my horse. It was during this time that I had a vision of those children. When I awoke my mount was gone and I ran until I ended up here. The rest I'm sure you already have heard. I tell you, she stalks me now as she has since her death."

"Who is she?" Miranda questioned, her interest in his tale growing.

"It is a long story." He responded, "and my time is short. Once more, thank you for the comfort that you provided me."

William turned and walked away from the window and sat down on the floor of his cell. Moments later, he could hear the girl's voice in the outer chamber of the jail, coupled with the sound of the guard's. The door opened. Light from the other room poured in and in strode one of the guards.

"Back away." He ordered in a booming voice, squinting into the cell which was still rich with shadows. William scooted back to the far wall of his cell as a small amount of bread was pushed through the bars and his water cup set within reach. The guard turned and walked back towards the door leading to the outer chamber of the jail, pausing at the doorway to speak.

"Better to get up and walk about to stretch those legs." He said smirking, "Then they will match your neck when we stretch it with a rope, tomorrow!"

The guard howled with laughter and was joined by his companion in the other room as the door shut. William picked up the bread. Stale, just as always. Not the warm, fresh bread that was brought by the sheriff's daughter, no meat. Just what was left over from the guard's meals from yesterday. Frustration overtook him as he threw the bread out of his cell and kicked through the bars, bouncing the cup across the room and spilling its contents.

With a deep sigh, William ran his hands through his greasy hair. He walked across his cell to his straw bed and sat down knowing that he was close to breaking.

"Hello?" a voice called in a hushed tone, from outside his window.

"Hello?" it repeated.

Could he not just be left in peace during the last day of his life? he wondered as he groaned, pushed himself to his feet, and walked to the window. He looked out the window into the alley to see the sheriff's daughter hiding in the shadows.

"I wish to hear your story, Mr. Bell." Miranda said, curiosity in her voice. "Think of it as a confessional, a chance to be heard. It may very well be your last."

William looked down at her pretty face. He wondered how old she was. Not yet twenty, he was sure. She seemed very much like a child, wanting to hear a story, his story.

"Well," she asked, "do you have a story to tell or not?"

It was this impatience that she presented with her curiosity that reminded him of his lost Isabella.

"Yes" William replied, amused at the feisty young woman, "I have a story, but for you to understand, I must start at the beginning, at my birth."

William Bell then began his strange tale.

"My birth mother was a servant to a prominent couple that lived on the outskirts of the bustling city of New York. The Master of the house was an old, cruel man, who was fueled by greed. He took advantage of my mother and violated her for years during her employment. If my mother, being an orphan herself, had rejected those advances she would have been cast out onto the streets where hunger, disease, and death were plentiful. Her only chance for survival was to allow the old man his way. It kept food in her belly and a roof over her head, for the cost of her body and dignity. This practice was not uncommon for masters and servants. The Lady of the house was a very compassionate and loving woman, well educated, and well mannered. She knew of her husband's infidelities but, turned a blind eye to it, as many houses do. She knew that if she spoke up, that her husband would banish my mother to the streets and she had truly grown to love the servant girl. The old man took his wife's acceptance of the situation as a sign of his rule over his house, however, nothing could be further from the truth.

The lady of the house grew even closer to my mother, comforting her when she could when the old man had been particularly brutal. Having never had children, she treated my mother as her own daughter. The old man was greatly offended by this and routine beatings began for the least imperfection in my mother's work. Somewhere in the midst of this terrible situation, my mother became with child, spawned by the Master of the house; James Bell.

When my mother realized this, she went to the Lady of the house, confiding in her. The Lady, had always sat passively by, but with a child's life now at stake, she funded my mother and sent her away in hiding. When the time drew near for my impending birth, Lady Bell journeyed to my mother's side to be with her. However upon arriving, she discovered that she was too late. My mother had died in childbirth and I had been cut from her stomach. Somehow, I had survived."

William paused and looked at the young woman, Miranda as she listened attentively.

"Yes," she pleaded, "Please continue!"

"Lady Bell," William continued his story, "took me as her own, the babe that she could never have, naming me after her brother, William, who died fighting against the British during the Battle of Brooklyn Heights. Upon our arrival back at the manor my father was furious at his wife. He had assumed that my mother had simply run away and he supposed that she had died in the streets with other trash of her kind. To find out that she was sent away and had his child, all unbeknownst to him, led him to despise me, even as a baby. In truth, I believe that were it not for my foster mother the old man would have murdered me in the crib where I lay just to be rid of this embarrassing mistake. I still remember his eyes from when I was a child, those horrible, hate filled eyes. There was no love for me at all. For my entire childhood he never once uttered my name. His most common calling for me was "boy". Just the thought of that old man makes my insides burn." William said, clinching the bars of the window. "All the while he rejected me. I tried ever harder to gain his approval, his attention....his acceptance of me. I just wanted my father to love me and I didn't understand why he did not. When I reached adolescence, a small boy in a large house with no playmates save for my foster mother, I took to typical rowdy behavior of children, which enraged my father. Often times I would purposely anger him just in order to receive a reaction from him, towards me. Of course, I would always dart to the safety of my mother to avoid his wrath.

One fateful day I made a mistake that would nearly cost me my life. I slipped into my father's chamber and curiously began exploring his personal belongings in his desk. I never noticed the figure standing in the corner of the room behind the thick drapes. Evidently my father had been standing at his chamber window, looking out at the streets below, when I entered the room. He heard me at the door and stepped into hiding. With my attention on the items in the desk drawer, he quietly came up behind me. His hands clasped around my throat before I realized that anyone else was in the room. I attempted to scream for my mother but my face was slammed into the desk. I remember the feeling of my own warm blood pouring down my face and running into my eyes turning my vision red, the salty taste as it ran into my mouth, the damned smell as I struggled to breath and sucked it into my nose. Time seemed to slow to a crawl as I turned, hurt and dazed, to face my father.

The look on his face was that of an animal, disgusted at the lack of struggle from its prey. He lashed out at me, striking me in the ear. After this there was no more sound just a distant roaring in my head. I broke free and tried to run but immediately fell. I tried to call out for my mother again. I felt my ribs break as he drove his boot into my side. I remember lying on my back, staring up at him, gasping for breath, and thinking that this was the end of my short life and I didn't even know why...but it was not to be. As the world began to grow dark, my consciousness slowly drifting away, I could see the old bastard fumbling with the belt of his trousers. I thank God that I passed out before the rape he committed.

I awoke in my mother's room, in her bed, beneath heavy blankets. My face was swollen and bruised. Every breath was a momentous struggle. The slivers of memories from the attack nauseated me. I remembered what he did to me.

My mother sat in a rocking chair beside me, weeping softly, never knowing that I had awoke and heard her prayer as she begged for forgiveness for placing a child in harm's way again, the first being my birth mother, whom I knew nothing of at that time. Upon hearing me stir she looked up and forced a smile. Her tears shown like rivers of silver in the delicate candle light.

'William,' she said to me gently, 'You must leave here, my son.' her voice breaking.

My jaw was badly swollen from my father's attack, leaving me unable to speak clearly as I struggled to protest. She placed one hand, gently, upon my arm to halt my agonizing movements, the other to her lips in a silencing gesture. She smiled again, blinking back her tears.

'You will go away. I have found a grand school that you will attend, far from the reaches of your father.' She exclaimed, with a forced smile and pride in her voice. You see, she had taught me to read and write, histories and sciences, and even some arts through private tutors, all at my father's chagrin. Why spend good money on what he saw as gutter riff raff? She had told me many times of distant universities and the opportunities that they offered. I dreamed of those universities often, of making a life for myself, of making my father proud. But that dream was gone. I never wanted to be in his presence again. I wished with all of my heart that he would die for what he had done to me.

I was to go away to one of these fabled universities. This dream that I carried in my heart was about to come true. The secrets of this world had always astonished me, for I desired knowledge in all things. Even through the painful swelling, I managed a pitiful smile to my mother, which caused the old woman to break down into tears of sadness mingled with tears of joy.

'I promise to write to you each day, my son,' she told me, her voice quivering. 'even if I must hire my own private army of messengers to deliver them! And you had better write me!'

I nodded, tears rolling down my face. I had never been so hurt, happy, and sad at the same time.

'Your belongings are already packed.' she said, 'You will depart within the week. My son, William, I am so proud of you. You have made me so happy and I love you so much.' She leaned forward and carefully embraced me and we wept together.

She held me until I drifted back to sleep, keeping constant vigil at my bedside until I was well enough to travel. Those long days we talked of my future and of things between a mother and a son. I was in constant fear that my father would return and possibly kill me, but that was not to happen. Finally the day came for me to leave. I remember the rain pouring down in great sheets as I walked down the manor steps to the waiting carriage, still wincing from my father's attack. This carriage would whisk me away to my new life.

My mother braved the storm, following me, professing her love for me again and again. Telling me of precautions that I should take to stay healthy, making sure that I had all of my belongings loaded in typical motherly fashion. Her tears were washed away by the rain and only the redness of her eyes betrayed her sadness. I loved this woman dearly, but it was time for me to depart this house lest I die there.

She stood waving, in the rain, as the carriage drew away. I glanced up at the upper level of the manor. In the window of my father's study I could see what I took to be him, standing there, staring down at me, burning with shame. I looked back to my mother, in the middle of the muddy road, still waving, her heart breaking, until she vanished from sight. That was the last time that I saw that house and my father for nearly twelve years.

My mother made good on her promise to write me often, though not at the pace of a letter each day as she had said, at least several times each month. She even visited a few times each year, when the weather and her health permitted. We would talk of my adventures at school, my studies while touring the campus, of the goings-on in New York, but never was my father mentioned. In time he became a childhood nightmare, a bogeyman that I had outgrown. Or at least, that's what I tried to convince myself of."

The sheriff's daughter looked up at William Bell, sorrow filling her eyes.

"What a terrible story, so sad." She responded to his pause.

Jolted from his recollection of the past he looked up to the sun, which shined brightly in the crisp blue sky. Noting to himself that it was fast approaching mid-day, judging by the position of the sun and the growling of his belly, William questioned the girl, "Are you not afraid of being caught here conversing with me? I'm sure that your punishment would be severe."

Looking down the alley both ways, Miranda shrugged her shoulders beneath her heavy coat.

"Everyone is occupied with daily chores, building the gallows, or preparing for tomorrow night's festivities." She replied. "No one will notice me here."

William noticed for the first time, the sound of hammering in the distance, the gallows being constructed.

"Festivities?" he asked, "What is the occasion?"

The look on Miranda's face answered his question as the grim finality of his predicament began to sink in.

"Oh, I see." He answered his own question, "I am the occasion."

Once more he forced a smile to the young girl. The sound of the outer chamber door swinging open caused William to spin about in his cell.

"You have been awful quite in here, Bell." the guard said eyeing, him. "Are you done with your whining and crying? Ready to take your punishment like a man? I doubt it. I'll bet you squeal like a pig when that rope goes around your scrawny neck tomorrow!"

William turned back to face the window. "I'm just trying to enjoy my last day on earth, with peace and quite."

"Enjoy it." the guard snorted, his words dripping in sarcasm, "Yes, enjoy your last day here, because tomorrow you will enjoy your first day in Hell!"

The guard spat into the cell at William then turned to leave, taking with him the bread and water that was to be his. When the door was fastened William stepped to the window once more to look down at the girl in the alley way, however, the alley was now empty. The Sheriff's daughter had vanished as if she had never been there.

Chapter 14

Brusion Beniot rode his horse into the outskirts of the farming village. Cold glares greeted him from each face that he encountered on the streets of the community. Brusion brought his steed to a stop before a group of men hard at work building what he knew to be the frame work of gallows.

"Greetings, friends" he spoke, "Where can I find the local constable?"

The men stopped working and looked up from their task.

"We are not you friends, stranger." One of them spoke, stepping down from the platform, "and we do not need any more outsiders around here."

Brusion looked at the man, steely eyed. He was accustomed to respect and considered stepping down to teach this discourteous man some manners, but he had more important business at hand than simple fisticuffs.

"My name is Brusion Beniot," he stated, his voice commanding attention, "I am tracking a man who has had a hand in killing at least eight people, one of them being my sister, and I have reason to believe that he is among you."

"Your killer?" one of the men replied, "tall and slender? Long yellow hair?"

"Bell!" Brusion spoke in excitement, "He is here?"

The man glared at him. "Oh, he is here alright. Locked safely away and awaiting his execution. Perhaps if your tracking skill had been better we would not have two dead children here."

"Children?!" Brusion exclaimed, "Dear God, what has he done now?!"

"Not him," chimed in one of the other men, "The girl that was with him. She killed the children and attacked an old woman. The murder weapon was found among the man, Bell's, belongings, but he won't tell where she is hiding. The children's father will return home this night after being sent for, and tomorrow at sun rise your killer will swing from his neck until dead!"

"And we will find his bitch and we will hang her as well!" chimed in another.

A broad smile crossed Brusion's face at the image of his family's bane hanging lifeless from these gallows. If only the price had not been so high. If only his horse had not had a misstep and broken its leg in the deep woods, costing him precious days, as he walked on foot to the nearest town to acquire a new mount. Though tragic as the cost was, it was time now to reap, through the death of others, William Bell's miserable life.

But here was the talk of Bell's female companion again, the one that the nuns had spoken of at the site of Bell's last massacre, the one that closely matched the description of his sister, Isabella, on the day of her funeral. Who could she be?

"Where is your jail?" Brusion asked, attempting to suppress the excitement in his voice. The workmen stared silently at Brusion Beniot, taking his measure, still untrusting.

"Sirs," Brusion spoke again, "I loved my sister dearly. Bell infiltrated my family in the guise of a tutor. He seduced my sister and turned her against us, her family. He ultimately betrayed and murdered her. We were powerless to save our own flesh and blood as he had taken her far away from the safety of her home. She died alone in the mud on the banks of a river, beaten to death by Bell's hand.

I have tracked this bastard, not for a bounty, but for the satisfaction of avenging my sister. For my father, who sits with a broken heart, mourning his daughter and for the innocent lives that he has claimed along the way. I, like the people of your village, have been wronged by this devil. I, like you, mourn for one that was taken needlessly and much too soon. I...." he paused, looking from one man to the other, "I, like you, deserve to see Bell atone for his sins. I wish to see him die." He stated bluntly.

Two of the workmen looked to each other, then to the third.

"I'll take you myself." one of the men spoke up, a bit more sympathetic.

Brusion nodded, "Thank you."

He nudged his horse, following the man down the earthen road as he stared back at the gallows slowly being erected. He noticed how the platform was unusually and purposely high, so that all could see, clearly, the spectacle of Bell's body as it danced upon the end of a rope. Brusion smiled again.

Soon, Brusion was in the streets of the small town. He followed his guide down the worn pathways between crude shops, stopping before a wooden building with iron bars covering the windows. A growing crowd of people stood in the streets outside the jail, waiting silently, whispering back and forth at his approach. Two men stood with muskets, one on each side of the only visible door to the jail.

Brusion dismounted and approached the jail, the crowd moving to allow passage to this massive stranger. He could feel the stares dissecting him fearfully as he stepped through the villagers and onto the old wooden porch, towering before the guards. One of the men quickly unslung his musket and pointed it in Brusion's direction. Brusion quickly took note on how the man handled the weapon. Hand grip too tight, shoulder position off, he was no soldier. Not even much of a hunter by the looks of his stance. But Brusion was not here to criticize the locals. He was here for the man just inside these walls; William Bell. Excitement flooded through him at the thought.

"I have need to speak with your sheriff" Brusion said, his excitement barely contained.

The guard aiming the rifle looked to his companion. Both were obviously intimidated by the presence of the large man. He nervously nodded, never dropping his shaking barrel from the direction of Brusion Beniot. Abandoning his position, the other guard opened the jail door and retreated inside to get the sheriff. Moments later the sheriff's burly form appeared in the doorway. The two imposing men eyed each other, each taking the other's measure. Brusion was taller, the sheriff wider. Neither man was willing to look away from the other's stare. After a prolonged, awkward silence, Sheriff Winston broke the silence.

"Who are you? What business do you have here?"

"I am Brusion Beniot," he answered, "a soldier in the American Army. I have traveled far from my home in New Orleans, to see to it that the man, William Bell, pays for my sister's death with his life."

Sheriff Winston looked over Brusion once more, noting the way the man carried himself. Confidence and strength was apparent in his stance.

"Your pistol first" The sheriff said, his gaze dropping to the butt of the handle which protruded just slightly from behind the young soldier.

Bruison slowly raised both hands as the sheriff motioned for the guard to take the stranger's weapon. The other guard, his musket still trained on Brusion, shook nervously. Carefully, the guard withdrew the pistol from Brusion's belt and handed it to Sheriff Winston. The sheriff inspected the pistol as he looked back to Brusion.

"Come inside." He said.

Brusion lowered his hands and entered the jail, ducking to fit through the doorway, followed by the sheriff who fastened and locked the door behind them. Once inside, Brusion told his long story to Sheriff Winston, who listened intently, from the point where William Bell entered his family home, to his sister's abduction, to the discovery of her body in New Orleans on the banks of the Mississippi River, to the near demise of his brother, and the death filled trail that he had followed on his quest for Bell.

Brusion's story finished, the sheriff then explained the details and circumstances around William Bell's arrival and the subsequent murders at the Taylor farm. Brusion sat in a mixed state of horror and disgust as he was told of a woman with midnight black hair wearing a red gown trimmed in gold who dragged a child into a brook and then beat and drowned her, of the same woman butchering the child's brother with a farming tool much like what was used back home on his families plantation. He was told of this woman, a woman fitting the final image of his sister as she lay in her coffin before her funeral, a woman that William Bell says stalks him from the grave, a woman that William Bell swears is Isabella Beniot. The sheriff left the room and when he returned he carried one of the bags that had been on Bell's horse when it was found on the Taylor farm the night of the murders. He reached inside and pulled forth a small book spattered with blood droplets. Brusion recognized the book and the hand writing upon it. This was his mother's journal. The one that he had seen her writing in so often as she neared her life's end. His sister had been obsessed with this book after finding it, never leaving it unguarded, constantly reading and rereading its pages. It must have been among her possessions when Bell murdered her. Rage flowed through Brusion's veins as Sheriff Winston then produced the sickle that was used in the boy's murder. Brusion took the tool, still covered in dried blood, and examined it carefully. The markings on the sickle caused an alien feeling of weakness to creep into his massive body, as his knees grew weak. This tool, he knew well. It came from his home, from the many tools that were used during the harvest.

"This proves nothing about my sister!" Brusion's voice boomed. "Bell could have easily stolen this from my home, as he stole my mother's journal from my sister when he killed her. I have no doubt that there is a woman with him, a part of his evil schemes, I have heard as much on my travels, but there is no possible way that it is my poor sister, Isabella. She died at his hand. I placed her in her coffin myself."

Sheriff Winston bowed his head, feeling sympathy for the large man. This man, Bell, awaiting his execution in the other room, had caused so much pain. Some people in the larger cities would demand that Bell go before a judge and stand trial for his crimes, but here in this rural area Nathanial Winston had heard all that he needed to hear. With the confirmation from Brusion Beniot that the weapon used to murder the children was indeed assessable to William Bell, that Bell was wanted for other murders, he was now convinced beyond doubt' that his decision was justified. The entire village supported it, no, demanded it. Bell would meet his end soon, after Landon Taylor arrived home. Then the search would continue for his female companion, whether she be what Bell swears is the dead, come back to the land of the living or a beast like monster in female form, as told by the murdered children's grandmother. Whoever, whatever, she was, he would not rest until he had her in shackles with a noose quick to follow. These crimes would not go unpunished and Bell was mere hours away from paying for his part in this. Yes, he was justified.

"I wish to see him." Brusion's deep voice brought the sheriff out of his thoughts. Brusion had need to see for himself that this devil, Bell, that he had pursued for all of these long months was indeed imprisoned here. To think that he was under the same roof made the big man's heart race.

With a nod, Sheriff Winston stood and motioned for Brusion to follow him. Beniot followed the sheriff across the room to the door that led to the holding cell. Pushing it open, the two men stepped into the room, scarcely lit by the afternoon sun peeking through the small cell window.

"Bell!" Brusion raged, "You devil! Step forward so that I can see your miserable carcass!"

"Brusion?!" a weak voice squeaked from the confines of the cell.

"Oh, it's me, you fiend! I swore to my father, on my mother and Isabella's grave, that I would track you to the ends of the earth to make you pay for your sins against my family! Here, I will complete that oath by watching your head snap from your body when you hang!"

"Brusion," William spoke meekly, "I know that you hate me and wish me dead. I know this. But I will not go to my grave without the truth being known to you. Whether you believe me or not is of no consequence. I love your sister, Isabella, this you know. Her death was a tragic accident and I had no part in it. I will never be over her loss, ever. These deaths here, and back at the convent, I swear that I am not responsible for them! Isabella calls to me. She comes to me in dreams and visions! She taunts me! She kills!" he exclaimed.

Anyone that tries to assist me or anything that I find comfort with is subject to her wrath! I swear to you that your sister walks among the living. The old woman, the children's grandmother, saw her wearing her red gown trimmed in golden threads! Isabella had such a gown!"

"Yes, you bastard!" Brusion roared, rushing forward to the bars, "She did have such a gown. We buried her in it!"

Brusion spat into the cell, striking William in the face.

"You dare profess your love for her and condemn her name with your cowardly actions? If I could lay hands on you now," he growled, reaching into the cell as Bell retreated to the far wall of the cell, "I would tear your limbs from your body while you still draw breath!"

"Enough." said the sheriff, placing a large hand upon Brusion Beniot's shoulder, "He will be dead soon."

Brusion brushed the sheriff's hand from his shoulder forcefully while still glaring at the cowering Bell, "May your putrid soul feed the hounds of Hell for all eternity, you miscreant."

Brusion spun on his heel and exited the room, followed by Sheriff Winston.

Chapter 15

William paced back and forth in his cell, his boot heels echoing throughout the jail. It was late afternoon now and his final hours were slowly slipping away. He was anxious before and now even more so at the thought of Brusion Beniot being in such close proximity. The bars of his cell now seemed weak in comparison to the hulking man that wanted nothing more in this world than his death.

"William!" a hushed voice called from the window at the back of his cell.

"William Bell!" the voice called again.

Walking to the window in his tired stride, William looked through the bars and saw the smiling face of the sheriff's daughter, Miranda, in the alley below.

"I apologize for my hasty retreat earlier but I heard someone approaching," she said, "I feared for your safety if my father found me conversing with you."

William chuckled lightly, "My dear, my safety is of no issue here. You speak now with but a breathing corpse. My time is nearly done."

"I am sorry." Miranda said softly. "I also fear angering him. I love my father dearly and do not wish to disgrace him by..." her words stopped.

"By befriending a killer?" William asked.

"No!" she said, "Yes!" she spoke, changing her response. "I don't know." She said finally. "I have been thinking of what you have told me, of your past. I...I want to hear the rest." She stammered, sinking back against the opposite wall to keep out of view of the gathered villagers at the front of the jail.

William forced a smile at her and then continued his tale.

"I excelled at the university, becoming amongst the best in my class. I tutored my classmates who struggled and found that it not only helped with my understanding of the material but that I had a gift for teaching myself. I truly loved my life there. In an effort learned from childhood I tried my hardest to make my professor proud of me, always volunteering in class, always going above and beyond what was asked for on assignments. I suspect it was a device used to attempt to fill the void of abuse and rejection from my father. However, unlike the heartache that I found at home, Professor Winkler accepted me with open arms, expressing admiration and giving praise, where deserved, often and without hesitation. He became a father figure to me, someone that I could talk to about the horrors of my youth, someone to confide in. I grew to love him. The months stretched to years.

I was respected at the university. I was wanted. Just as everything in my life was falling into place I received the news that would crumble the foundations of my world and send it toppling to the ground once more. Late one sunny, spring afternoon, while returning from an advanced scientific lecture, I found Professor Winkler awaiting me at my dormitory. His expression was grim as he stood there staring at me through his spectacles.

'William,' he spoke somberly, 'It's your mother. She is gravely ill...dying. You should go to her at once.'

A feeling of dread overtook me, my knees weakening. My mother, the sweet woman who had saved me from the clutches of my abusive father, was dying? I had never let the thought of a world without her cross my mind. I just could not comprehend it. I rushed to my room and assembled my belongings. Within the hour I was in a carriage heading back to Bell Manor in New York, heading home. The next week was a drawn out experience as I traveled the great distance, mourning a woman that wasn't yet dead, or at least, so I hoped. The times of my youth played out over and over in my head leaving my stomach in knots. The last time that I saw my father and what he did to me, these thoughts tortured me. In my mind I was that small child again, defenseless against him, the man whom had nearly killed me.

At last the city of New York stretched out before me with its tall buildings, crowded streets, and grey skies. Hours later, after navigating the buggy filled roads, the carriage came to a halt in front of the old Bell manor. The rain beat down as I stepped out onto the muddy street. It was as if the scene of my departure had remained the same throughout all of these years. The rain still fell in great sheets, the house still stood ominous as ever, and a dark figure stood in the window of my father's study, watching me...hating me. The only thing missing was my mother, smiling in the down pour, the rain disguising her tears as she waved goodbye. This time, however, it was the rain hiding my tears as I had come to say goodbye to my mother, forever.

Taking a deep breath and dragging my bags, I forced my body up the front steps to the grand doors. The lion statues, which flanked either side of the steps, stood with their mouths open in an eternal roar, just as I remembered them. I pressed open the large door and stepped into the great hall of the manor. I set my bags down and immediately ascended the stairway to my mother's chamber. There were no candles to light the way leaving the stairs dark and obscure, as if my mother's impending demise had ushered all light from the house, never to return. Unwanted childhood memories overcame me with each familiar creak of the steps, with every remembered painting. Then I was standing at my mother's chamber. Soft light escaped from the crack beneath the door. I said a silent prayer that I wasn't too late and then entered the room.

I tried to be strong. I did, but the sight of my beloved mother lying so still in her bed broke me. I rushed to her side, dropping to my knees and crying like a child. Her head was wrapped in bandages, blood seeping through them. Her face was swollen and her fever was high. The handmaid, a young girl that was unfamiliar to me, took me by the arm and pulled me to my feet. She explained that my mother had slipped and tumbled down the stairs, striking her head on the stone floor at the bottom. She had fallen into a deep sleep and had not woken since. I sat with my mother the entire night, holding her hand. Whispering in her ear of the days when I was a child and she would take me into the city for all sorts of adventures. I told her of my exploits at the university since her last visit. I bathed her head with cool rags and did what I could to comfort her as her breathing slowed. It was nearing dawn when I drifted off to sleep for but a moment. When I woke, my beautiful, loving, mother had passed from this world, quietly, still holding my hand.

I wept and said a silent prayer. I then stood and walked across her bedroom and stepped out into the hallway. I had to get out of this house. The walls seemed to be closing in and I couldn't catch my breath. As I rushed to the stairs, there, blocking the way with a scowl of disgust on his face, stood my father. His grey hair hung long about his balding head.

'Welcome home, boy!' he rasped

'Father…' I spoke, my blood running cold. I didn't know what to say.

'If she is dead,' he mocked, 'there will be no funeral. I can stomach her stench within these walls no longer.'

I was stunned by the cruelty of his wretched words.

'Father,' I questioned him in disbelief, 'How could you? She was your wife! She loved you!'

'No, you little fool!' he yelled back at me, '"he betrayed me! She betrayed me for you! She told me that she had sent you away to an orphanage but instead she lied to me and squandered my fortunes on your so called education!'

'Why, father?' I asked, 'Why do you hate me so?'

A brief smile spread across his wrinkled face, the only time that I ever remember seeing him smile, as he rapped the silver tip of his cane on the guard rail of the stairs.

'Hate you?' he asked coldly, 'You see yourself in too kind of a light, boy. There are no words for what I feel for you. I sent for you myself, because you see, she didn't just betray me. She betrayed you too, boy. She wasn't even your true mother.'

His words stung more than any physical abuse that he had ever subjected me to.

'Your mother,' he continued, 'was nothing more than a common whore whom I took a fancy to and gave her a job cleaning my boots. She cursed me with your existence. You ripped her apart when you were born, killing her. My wife, the woman that you call mother, yes, I did love until you came between us. When she brought you here she became nothing more than a servant to your every mewling whelm.

After all of these years the truth finally was revealed to me. I became aware of your whereabouts and that my riches were slowly being drained for a bastard child who may or may not be my offspring! I confronted your "mother" about you and of course she defended you as always. Well, this time my kindness was pushed too far beyond its limit! Look into my eye's you miserable fool. I bashed in her skull with my cane!' He said, striking the silver tip against the palm of his open hand, 'and then I threw her down the stairs! The crimson spot where your bags lie,' he said, pointing with his cane, 'is where her body came to rest.'

Looking over the rail I could see, in the dark corridor below, the gruesome spot where my mother's blood had pooled. I collapsed against the rail, all strength leaving me. Everywhere I looked I could see my mother's face. She had been such a loving soul and this monster, my father, had killed her and brought me here just to gloat about his actions, to crush me this one final time, but I was no longer a child as I had been during his last assault on me. I was now a man of twenty four years and he was old. Old and sick. I could hear the wheezing with each labored breath that he took. My grief and rage overtook me. For once, in his presence, I was strong. I lunged for him. With an inhuman howl I was upon him, grabbing him by the lapels of his coat and forcing him back over the rail high above the stone floor. I gritted my teeth in anger as I peered into his grey eyes. I wasn't sure if it was fear or surprise that had gripped the old man while he stared up at me, in silence, his life in my hands.

'You are a coward, boy!' he rasped, regaining his composure, somewhat. 'Kill me!'

I shook with emotion. He deserved death. I wanted to give it to him, the one gift from his son that he could be proud of. The gift that would see me imprisoned or possibly hanged for. The old man knew he was dying and this would be his way of making sure that I would suffer for the rest of my life, by taking my revenge. I wanted to end him, but I couldn't. My mother had tried too hard to free me from the grasp of this pathetic monster. I spun him around and sent him sprawling to the floor, his breath exploding from his body as he landed.

'Goodbye, father. No one will miss you when you die.' I said as I turned to flee down the stairs, away from this accursed place.

'You are not my son!' I heard the old man screech as he pushed himself from the floor and hurtled wildly towards me.

Instinctively, I stepped to the side and the old man tumbled past me down the steep staircase. The horrible sounds of his scream and of his body smashing against the wooden stairs echoed throughout the mansion. With a sickening thud his body came to rest at the bottom of the stairs, his neck twisted at an unnatural angle, eyes and mouth wide in disbelief. Dead.

I stood upon the stairs, not believing what had happened. Was he really dead? Was the beast from my nightmares really dead at my feet?

'Master Bell?' I heard the handmaid call from the floor above.

I looked up to see her staring down at me, on the stairs, and my dead father below. I was overwrought with emotion and dashed down the stairs past the old man's twisted body, grabbing my bags as I pushed my way out the doors and into the waiting storm.

'Boy!' I thought I heard the old man yell over the roar of the thunder and the screams of the servant as I ran to carriage house, but it must have just been the wind. I hitched one of the horses to the carriage and loaded my bags quickly. I climbed onto the carriage seat and drove the animal out onto the streets, fleeing my childhood home that day, like so many years before, only this time I would never return. Shivers went down my spine as I glanced for the final time at Bell manor. In the upstairs window of my father's study, I swear I saw a figure standing there, watching me, hating me.

I wondered as I fled New York, how long it would be before the authorities were on my trail? It seemed that my father's scheme had come to fruition, with his death. Surely with the sounds of our scuffle and my hasty retreat, his death looked much more than the accident that it was. I dared not return to the university. That would be the first place that would be searched. I desperately desired council with my mentor, Professor Winkler. He knew my mother well and also knew of the evil deeds of my father. Perhaps he could advise me of what I should do. If anyone would believe me, it would be him. Two days travel from New York, I came across a small farm where I traded the carriage for a saddle for my horse so that I could move faster. I then continued my journey south.

I had been to Professor Winkler's home, which was only a few miles from the university, several times, as his guest for dinners and social parties. That would be the most probable place to meet with him in secret. With the entire foundation of my life, my being, cracking and crumbling, I hid in the woods near his home, waiting for the sun to go down and providing me with my blanket of cover. I remember hearing the approach of a rider on the dark road and being able to make out the recognized voice of my friend as he sang, poorly, one of his favorite ballads: Escape of Old John Webb.

'So they stole them a horse and away did ride, and who what they rode gallantly,

Until they came to the river bank, to the river runnin' wild and free!', he sang, his voice rising over the footfall of his horse.

He trotted past the spot where I hid, watching him, never realizing that there was another soul around. I move out onto the road on foot, following him through the gates leading up to his sizable abode. As the professor dismounted his horse, I approached him.

'Professor Winkler,' I called to him, interrupting his song.

'What?!' he yelled back, startled, 'Who's there?'

'William, sir.' I answered, 'William Bell.'

As I drew closer I could smell wine, heavy, on Professor Winkler's breath. He must have stopped by the local tavern on his way.

'William, lad!' he replied, drunkenly, 'How is your mother?!'

'My mother is dead.' It was the first time that I had to utter those words and my heart broke. I ran forward and threw my arms around his shoulders and sobbed like a child.

'There, there, my poor boy.' he said, my words sobering him up somewhat, as he patted my back. 'Let's get you inside and fed.'

'Professor, there's more.' I cried, 'My father is dead as well, and it is believed that I killed him. He tried to attack me on the stairway outside of my mother's chamber and when I moved out of his way he fell to his death. I panicked and fled. My retreat was witnessed by one of his servants. I don't know what to do now.'

'Oh, dear,' he said, pushing out of my embrace so that he could look me in the eyes, 'I see your plight! You were a fool to come back here! You have to get as far away from here as quickly as you can!'

'I don't know where to go!' I pleaded, lost as to what I should do.

Professor Winkler stood looking over his spectacles and stroking his chin, as was common for him when he was deep in thought.

'New Orleans!' Professor Winkler exclaimed, 'It's an extraordinary place and so far from here! You will be safe there! Come lad, let's get you a few things and get you on your way!'

Within an hour I had said my goodbyes to my mentor and was back on my horse with some supplies and enough funds to see me to my destination. I had a crude map directing me south west into the Tennessee area, once there I traveled to Nashville. The long weeks were quite as I tried to maintain my secrecy, keeping to myself. From Nashville I followed a common trail known as the Natchez Trace down into the Mississippi territory. The trace had been developed by soldiers at first, and later by ordinary citizens. It was assessable by wagon, with Inns and trading stands being found sparsely along the way. It is known by another name, however, for those who travel it; the Devil's Backbone, due to its remoteness, terrible conditions, and the constant threat of robbers and highwaymen. I can assure you that the name is well warranted. That summer of travels, the weeks spent on that trail, were some of the most miserable of my life. Covered in constant sweat I spent much of that time besieged by all manner of biting insects, dodging snakes, and wary of beasts in between stops. I remember several times hearing the distant sound of the Choctaw drums being played from the trace as I neared their settlements. These were the dangers that I was privy to on my quest for freedom.

Eventually I found my way to a small city on the banks of the Mississippi River called Natchez, where the trail originated from. I was there only long enough to trade my horse for passage aboard a boat down river, to New Orleans.

New Orleans was such a place different from any that I had ever seen, much different from New York. And I was the furthest from the curse of Bell manor than I had ever been. I missed my mother, I missed Professor Winkler, and I missed my beloved university. But all of that was a part of another life now, a life that I was forced to leave far behind me.

Now within the streets of this strange city, so new to me, I could become a new person, any person. I was only tied to my past by memories. However new beginnings are difficult. I had no friends here, no place to stay, and my funds were nearly exhausted. For a time, I found shelter in an abandoned building that had been heavily damaged by a previous fire. It wasn't the comforts of the university, but it had a small area near the back of the structure that still had its roof and walls. It kept me dry and protected from the elements at least. I worked odd jobs in exchange for food at any place that would allow me. I would make myself as presentable as possible and venture into the more well-to-do neighborhoods where I presented myself as a tutor for hire. As my luck would have it, it wasn't long before I had found a family interested in my services, the wealthy and somewhat famous Beniot family that lived a day's ride from the city. That night, in a tavern in the heart of New Orleans, I made a decision that would forever alter my life by accepting the position."

Chapter 16

"I remember how nervous and excited I was on that mid afternoon as I approached the Beniot plantation inside the buggy that the family had provided for me. I beheld a massive mansion with huge sugar cane fields stretched out about the estate. The buggy made its way down the earthen road and turned off onto the lengthy cobblestone path leading up to the entrance of the mansion. Oh, how I wished Professor Winkler could have been there to offer me words of encouragement as he always did back at the university, but alas, I was on my own.

Huge oak trees with limbs spidering off in all directions and adorned with Spanish moss lined either side of the pathway. The vast tree branches met and intertwined high above, forming an arching awning of nature. The plantation was certainly a splendor to view. Eight massive columns stood at the front of the mansion, reaching to the third floor. Meticulously shaped hedges and other landscaping decorated the grounds, divulging a large slave presence for the necessary upkeep of the grounds and farming of such an area. The carriage came to a stop before the mansion, giving a merciful end to the bumpy ride. Rising from the seat, I stepped out onto the stone walkway and stretched my stiff and aching body. The fellow driving the carriage hopped down and began removing my belongings from the back of the buggy, placing them beside me on the walkway. I breathed deeply as I turned in place, marveling at these new surroundings that were soon to become my new home for the duration of my tutorial services. The beauty of this place, with its majesticness, captivated me.

The blood flooded back to my lower extremities, sending what felt like thousands of needles to prick at my body. Gathering my belongings as best I could I walked awkwardly up the marble steps, my legs still not feeling quite my own. Stepping onto the porch, I saw that the ceiling above was painted with a mural of British and American soldiers locked in a battle scene from what must have been the fabled Battle of New Orleans, which occurred a few years earlier. I had heard all about this bloody battle back at the university and here it was, represented in its full glory. The elements of the Louisianan climate had already begun to take its toll on the artwork, with parts of the painting succumbing to mold and small areas chipping away. Even in this state it was still breathtaking.

I stepped to the large, ornately carved, wooden doors. Roses and twisting vines were etched, with painstaking precision, into the wood. I paused for a moment, setting down my baggage and straightening my garments and such, attempting to make myself presentable. I then reached forward and took the heavy iron door knocker in my hand which was molded in the form of a lion's head, briefly reminding me of the statues at Bell manor. Letting go, the weight of the object slammed against the door, alerting those inside the mansion of my arrival.

Long moments passed as my insides twisted with excitement, anticipating the opening of the door. I could hear heavy footfalls approaching from within. The hinges creaked and groaned beneath the labor of the weight that they bore as the door slowly opened. Standing in the doorway was a hulk of a man with piercing green eyes. He stood there, glaring at me, his pose as stone-like as the pillars supporting the mansion. His demeanor was immediately unsettling and I found myself either unable or unwilling to hold his stare. After a few awkward moments of silence I managed to draw enough nerve to speak.

'Hello, sir,' I stammered, 'I am William Bell, the tutor that was requested from New Orleans. I am very pleased and honored to...', but I didn't get the chance to finish my greeting, the practiced one that I had gone over countless times in my head on my journey there. The large fellow interrupted me.

'My father has been expecting you.' he said in a voice absent of feelings, 'Bring your belongings and follow me. I will show you to your quarters so that you may freshen up before dinner.'

With no further words he turned and walked away leaving me standing there, struggling with my baggage, a foolish grin upon my face. A box or bag tucked away under each arm and a stack of bound text books, mine from the university, piled higher than safely possible, I hurried behind the young man who seemed indifferent to my dilemma. Sweat broke out on my brow as I tried desperately to keep up with the man's pace. The end result was never really in doubt. With muscles cramping beneath the prolonged strain and pride unwilling to allow me to ask for assistance, I soon found myself beneath an avalanche of books, papers, and my other personal items.

The young man ahead of me turned and watched, amused, as I scrambled about like a buffoon trying to gather all of my belongings into a manageable pile that I could carry. He must have felt some sympathy for me as he reached down, taking my two largest packs, and hoisted the load up easily, further making me feel ridiculous. Grabbing my last few items and standing, I tried to retain my last shred of dignity.

'Thank you.' I said, unsure how to address the young fellow.

'Jacob.' He replied as he turned and continued on his way, 'My name is Jacob Beniot.'

'Ah, yes!' I said, excited at what I hoped was an ice- breaking opportunity, 'Jacob! Thank you Jacob!' however, my attempt at striking up a friendly conversation fell upon deaf ears. It was fairly evident that Jacob Beniot did not desire my company here. I was walking into a family of soldiers and this one was following the orders that were given to him by his father, orders that I wasn't so sure that he liked. After following Jacob up a tall flight of stairs and down several long hallways he, finally, came to a stop. It was only at this point that I was able to focus on the incredible interior of this magnificent house, as I had been hopelessly distracted by my earlier predicament. The Ceilings in this hallway were very high, with ornate trim around the walls. Fine paintings adorned the hallway at various locations and a vibrant red carpet runner covered much of the wooden floors. The smell of rose petals was faint upon the air in the house, much like the lingering aroma of a favorite loved one that hangs about after they have just departed from a room, forcing you to notice their absence.

Jacob pushed open the door to the room that would serve as my personal chamber for the coming months. He dropped my baggage just inside the entrance, the twin thuds sounding out upon the wooden floors.

'A servant will be sent for you when my father is prepared to dine.'

That being said he turned and walked out of the room and back down the hallway, leaving me feeling lost and alone in this big house, but also feeling excited! More excited than I could ever remember!

'Here,' I said to myself looking about my room and nodding, 'within these walls I will lay the first bricks of the foundation on which my new life shall be built!'

So far away from New York, where no one knew me or my past, I was ready to recognize a dream that I held from my time at the university;

to become a teacher myself. Professor Winkler had aided me so, in all ways of my life, I could only hope to be as great and inspiring an influence on someone else and here stood the opportunity.

This was to be my very first steps in finding myself. How naïve I was."

"Do you tire of my story yet?" William asked, looking down at Miranda as he momentarily halted his revelry.

"No." she responded with a smile, looking carefully down the alleyway to assure her concealment, "Please, go on."

"I walked about my room, exploring." William continued, "It was much like the rest of the mansion that I had seen, which in many ways reminded me of Bell manor, my childhood home, large and extravagant, filled with fine things that most people would only hear about in stories. There was a fireplace against the far wall of the room with several logs stacked upon the hearth, ready for use. A large cherry wood desk was placed before a tall arching window overlooking the back garden area. Oil paintings of mountainous landscapes decorated the walls. A tall doorway across from the fire place led to my bedroom. Inside were several elegant chest of drawers lining the walls and a huge four post bed. More masterfully crafted paintings were hung high about the room. On a small stand near the foot of the bed I found a porcelain basin and pitcher filled with cool, fresh water. I threw myself back upon my bed like a child, a huge smile upon my face, as I sank into the soft bedding. After many moments of relaxing I got up and dragged my bags that contained my clothing into the bedroom. I retrieved my best dining suit from my belongings and began to undress. I bathed quickly, using the water basin, and dressed in my finest. Then, as I awaited my summons to dinner, I started unpacking the rest of my belongings and putting them away.

When I had finished I went back into my study. It was growing darker in the room as the afternoon gave way to evening. I peered out the large window at the setting sun, a distant red ball of fire slowly melting into the horizon. I assumed that I would have been sent for before now. Looking about the room once more and spurred on by the rumbling in my gut, I stepped out into the long hallway trying to remember my way back to the entrance hall.

After a few twists and turns I found my way back to the stairway that led down to the front of the mansion. The entire house was growing dark now and I was overcome with the strangest feeling that I was being watched, no, a better word would be stalked. My paranoia would not plague me long as a deep voice spoke from the shadows behind me.

'You were told that you would be sent for.' A familiar voice said.

I spun, startled, to face Jacob Beniot.

'Have you been following me?' I asked, 'Watching me?'

I could sense the agitation in his voice as he answered, 'Sir, this is my home and all within its walls belong to me and my family. Here, I roam where I like...'

He moved several steps forward, standing before me with an uncomfortable closeness, almost threatening, yet there were no obvious outward signs of aggression.

'And I watch what I wish.' Jacob continued, pausing for a moment as if to allow me time to understand his meaning, what I took as a veiled threat.

I stood silent, staring at the big man and thinking that if Jacob was the student that I had been hired to tutor here, then my stay at the Beniot plantation may be a short one indeed. A smirk crossed his face. Satisfaction at seeing me unnerved, I suppose.

'My father awaits your company in the dinning hall.' Jacob said, breaking the uneasy silence. He stepped past me and ventured down another hallway. I collected my senses for a moment, telling myself that I would not be intimidated, which didn't work by the way, and followed down the hall to the dinning area.

Flashes of orange light played upon the walls as we stepped to the door of the dinning hall. Shadows danced in the orange light, reflected from the fire blazing in the hearth, as it fought away the first touch of chill in the early fall air. The sweet and welcomed smell of the prepared meal flooded my senses, enticing my growling belly and causing my mouth to water. I stood beside Jacob, unsure if I should enter or wait until an invitation was offered. As if sensing my uncertainty, and taking a bit of satisfaction in it, Jacob stared blankly at me. With a deep breath and a forced smile I took the initiative, nodded my thanks to Jacob, and stepped into the dinning hall. The spacious rectangular room had high, towering, ceilings and two tall arching windows that were spaced generously apart. In the area between the two windows was a large oil painting of a beautiful woman. Her hair was painted as black as sackcloth and her skin was the color of a china doll's. It must have been obvious that my attention was captured by the beauty in the painting as the patriarch of the Beniot family spoke to me from his place at the head of the long banquet.

'That is my lovely wife, Lida.' his rough voice echoed through the room, 'Beautiful, is she not?'

The old man stared at me with his steely gaze, while one hand stroked his thin grey beard. An unsightly scar, no doubt from battles past, snaked down one side of his face vanishing into his facial hair. A thin sheen of sweat was upon his balding pate, a condition of being seated so close to the fireplace.

'Yes, sir,' I stammered, turning to meet the old man's scrutiny, 'very beautiful. Will she be joining us for dinner?'

'I'm afraid that she is no longer of this world,' the old man replied, pain in his voice, 'but I placed that painting of her here in this hall so that she will always be with me when I dine.'

'I'm terribly sorry, sir!' I spoke, feeling a fool for dredging up sad memories, 'I had no idea.'

'Come, sit down Mister Bell. We have much to discuss about our arrangement.' He said, obviously wanting to shift the tides of the conversation.

I took my place at the end of the elegant dining table as servants brought forth the evening meal. A rack of lamb was placed before me. The savory smell of the meet forced a final rumble from my impatient stomach. Seasoned potatoes and greens were heaped upon my plate and a red wine was poured into my glass. I looked at the old man over the silver candelabra that sat near the middle of the table, as he sipped his wine, watching me.

'Will we dine alone?' I asked looking back to the door that I entered but finding that Jacob had vanished.

'Yes.' The elder Beniot replied. 'My children shall take their meals in their own chambers this evening so that we will have privacy to discuss the matters at hand.'

The old man studied me closely as his finger played around the edge of his wine glass. 'Where did you complete your studies, Mister Bell?'

'Well, sir,' I answered after swallowing the small bit of lamb that I had chewed, 'I completed my studies at a small university near Williamsburg, Virginia last year. I studied under Professor Danial Winkler for many years there. I was placed in a position, by several of the professors, where I tutored many of my colleagues. I had thought of pursing a career at the university.'

'What changed your mind?' he asked, 'How do you find yourself so far away from your home?'

I spoke, 'My mother died, leaving me with mostly painful memories and no ties left for the area. I had heard my professor speak of New Orleans and was captivated by his tales so I decided to venture out and see it for myself. Once I arrived I fell in love with the city, however my skill set is limited I'm afraid, to peddling knowledge, therefore I began offering up myself as a tutor.'

'I understand, Mister Bell.' He said, his eyes drifting to the painting of his beloved wife, 'Grief has a way of driving us away from things that we once loved. Forgive my son, Jacob, of his abrasive ways. He has reservations about a stranger coming into our home. He and my oldest son, Brusion, are very protective over your soon to be student.'

Taking a swig of my wine to wash down another bite of food I asked, 'And who is to be my student?'

'My daughter,' he replied, 'My Isabella.'

I was instantly relieved to find that Jacob was not to be my student.

'My Isabella,' the old man continued, 'She is not of the world that I and her brothers are. We are soldiers, hard men, not the company suited for a young woman whose interest lies in arts and poetry, writings and sciences. When her mother passed away, the pain left by her absence had a profound effect on her, on all of us. It was especially hard on Isabella, growing up here, the only female left in this family of men. It was hard on me. I knew nothing of raising a girl. She wanted to leave home after her mother's death to escape the heartache that her memories bring her at every turn in this old house. She submerged herself in her books and writings.

It was there that her love of the arts developed and her thirst for knowledge grew. She was always trying to find a way to leave us. Just a few years ago it was to attend an academy in Massachusetts.'

'Ah, yes, Bradford Academy.' I interrupted, 'The first in Massachusetts to admit women!'

'Yes, I was able to discourage her from that decision, and the Litchfield Academy after that, but now Paris is on her mind.' The old man answered, a bit of annoyance in his voice, obviously not used to people speaking out of turn in his presence, 'To be honest Mister Bell, I have no desire to have my daughter so far from home. Here, I know that she is safe. Here, I can protect her. I'm not sure that this old heart,' he said, thumping himself on his chest, and producing a fatherly smile, 'could survive the distance if Isabella were to leave her home. You see, Mister Bell, we have tried tutors before in hopes that my sweet daughter would satisfy her thirst for knowledge here instead of traveling away from home to do so, but all of them have failed, so far. Not to insinuate that they were inadequate at their jobs, but my Isabella... She is a rambunctious, stubborn soul, much like her mother was. She is captivated by the romance of poems and plays, arts and writings that are not of the normal variety. Many of the other tutors did not understand her love of such things and tried to convince her that the trials of youth were clouding her judgement on what is important, what is true art, and that wisdom escapes her. Needless to say, her incorrigible behavior and unrelenting arguments defending her beliefs have ended all past tutorial arrangements with failure.'

'I understand, sir.' I spoke, making sure this time that the old man was finished speaking.

'Make sure that you do.' He warned. 'My daughter is of the most important things in this world to me and my sons, a living embodiment of my wife. You are to tutor her in her academic studies, humor her concerning her taste in art, change her mind when she speaks of abandoning her home. These are the only tasks that have been set before you. Is this understood, Mister Bell?'

'Yes, Mister Beniot.' I answered, 'I understand perfectly. I will do all that is in my capability to insure Miss Beniot's scholarly advancements meet your approval and that your other wishes are fulfilled.'

'Good.' He replied, 'Let us finish our meal.'

We ate in mostly silence with the occasional question about my past coming up. It wasn't as much an interview as it was an interrogation, but with the safety of his daughter at stake, I could easily understand his concern. With dinner finished and the servants cleaning up, the old man looked to me, appearing to be searching for the right words to say. A broad smile spread across his face and the look of the brooding soldier was gone, replaced by what could have been mistaken for a comforting, grandfather like expression, but he was overtaken by a violent coughing fit. The wracking coughs seemed to send his body into spasms with their intensity, as he gasped for breath. I jumped to my feet, alarmed, as the sounds of his coughing fit echoed throughout the dinning hall.

'Sir?!' I said, 'Are you well?'

Without looking at me, old man Beniot motioned for me to be seated. Hesitantly, I did, as his coughing seemed to subside a bit. The old man wiped his mouth with his napkin, revealing bright crimson stains. Taking a deep, labored, breath he looked at me with a stern gaze.

He spoke, his voice rasping, his breath labored, 'Isabella thinks that she is to leave for Paris, but I have brought you here to offer her the education that she desires and to change her mind. You will be rewarded handsomely for your services. My daughter must remain here with me, Mister Bell. So, I implore you, do not fail me.'

The old man turned and tossed the blood covered napkin into the blazing hearth. Turning back to me, he forced a smile.

'Welcome to Beniot Plantation, young man.' He said as he rose from the table. 'Whatever you find that you may need do not hesitate to ask. I hope that we will all enjoy your time here, with us. Good evening.'

The old soldier walked, gingerly, across the room, seeming still out of sorts from his coughing spell and out one of the doors, retiring for the night. I sat a bit longer indulging the wine and enjoying the fire, thinking over the old man's words, eager to meet my student, eager to begin."

Chapter 17

"I was jarred from my intense thoughts by shouts from the hallway. I could make out the sounds of an argument between a man and woman, as their footsteps sounded out on the wooded floors, disclosing their approach. The young woman from the painting stepped through the doorway and into the dinning room, a small bound book in her hand, her long black hair flowing around her as she shook her head in anger, screaming back at the entrance, oblivious to my presence.

'Why do you all seek to keep me locked away here in this house like some fairy tale princess, brother?' she asked. 'I had made plans to leave for Paris last month and find now, on the eve of my departure, that I will not be allowed to go? I am a grown woman! You cannot keep me prisoner here for my entire life!'

A large form followed the young woman, stepping into the doorway carrying a musket in one hand and the carcass of a waterfowl by the neck, in the other. He wore muddied clothing from the day's hunt. Jacob, I had thought at first, but I was wrong. This was the eldest son of the Beniot clan, Brusion, which meant that the angry young woman was my proposed student; Isabella Beniot.

'Isabella,' the large man spoke, 'Your words are not fair. Our father…'

Isabella quickly cut her brother's words short.

'Fair?!' she yelled, her jaw clinching in fury, 'Endless bartering for my future? A never ceasing parade of idiots brought here to insult my passions? Or perhaps it is fair for our father to lock me away here so that he may keep me as his own personal treasure until I am an old woman! I am his daughter, not his wife!'

'That is enough, sister!' Brusion scolded, 'He loves you and only desires what is best for you.'

'He loves pride and his damned honor!' she countered, 'And if you were not so much his puppet you would see my point, but you have lived his life for so long now that you have no life of your own. Had I been born a boy, I, too, would have been dragged down the soldier's path.'

The veins in the large man's neck tensed and strained against his skin as his cheeks reddened with anger. He clinched his fists as he responded to his sister's verbal onslaught while she stood, scowling at him. Isabella was able to touch nerves in an emotional serenade, as talented, in her own way, as you are when you touch the strings of your harp.

'You ungrateful, little, brat!' Brusion spat, as it seemed he contemplated physically escalating the argument.

At this point the arguing siblings became aware of their audience. Isabella looked at me, a brief expression of amusement on her face, while her brother held me in his icy stare. Now growing accustomed to the feeling of discomfort within the walls of the Beniot house, I spoke first.

'Hello,' I said, forcing a weak smile, 'I am William Bell, the latest offering from your parade of idiots. I will be residing here, in your grand home while offering my tutelage.'

'Another one?!' Isabella asked, flabbergasted, as she turned back to Brusion.

For a long moment Brusion remained quiet as he looked at me. Slowly, his teeth unclenched. His face, previously contorted with anger, relaxed and the sound of air rushing into his massive lungs, as he breathed deeply, calming himself, could be heard.

'I am Brusion Beniot.' He said, formally introducing himself, 'I bid you welcome to our home, Mister Bell.'

Glancing over to his sister, Brusion continued, 'We apologize for what you saw. We thought ourselves alone.'

'He apologizes.' Isabella remarked, holding her brother's stare, 'I, however, see no reason to recant my statements, unless I apologize for my families closed minded ignorance.'

Brusion looked to me and bid me goodnight as he turned and thrust the dead bird into his sister's arms. Isabella stood, shaking in anger as Brusion walked out of the dinning hall. With a yell, she hurled the dead animal through the doorway and into the hall after him.

'Take your damned bird with you!' she screamed as she turned and walked towards me, extending her arm. I rose from my seat and reached out to take the hand of the approaching beautiful and angry young woman. A smile spread on her face. She reached past me, lifting my wine glass from the table to her lips and drank deeply before placing the empty glass in my still extended hand.

'I hate hunting.' she said, a twinkle in her eyes, 'Don't you?'

I stood there awkwardly, not getting the chance to respond as she spun around and darted towards the doorway.

'Tomorrow, perhaps we will see what it is that you think you have to teach me. Don't bother unpacking your things, Mister Bell.' she said, kicking the body of the fowl harshly, 'You won't be here long.'

And with that she was gone and I stood there holding my empty glass in the fire light, feeling that failure was inevitable and also not an option. I believe that I fell in love with her that night, with her fire, her passion, her tragedy. I placed my glass on the table, stepped out of the dinning hall as the servants moved in to tidy up, and returned to my room for a restless night of troubled sleep, dreaming of my dead father who hated me and the beautiful girl that had no desire for me to be there.

I awoke the next morning and with the aid of servants, found my way to the study room, where Isabella's daily lessons would be taught. With eager anticipation, I awaited my young student. After a long night of twisting and turning in my bed I had decided that I would win over this angry young woman. I was to be her tutor, yes, but just as Professor Winkler had become more than just my teacher, I would have to be more for Isabella. She needed more.

It wasn't long before she arrived, her lengthy hair held back by a piece of black ribbon, her long blue dress sweeping the floor as she walked, the same book from the night before carried in her hands. She was indeed a thing of beauty. I understood immediately, her father's concern of her being away from his protection. Her face was remarkably perfect, an angel's, seemed carved from marble with her pale complexion. Her rose petal colored lips pressed together with a natural pout. Her eyes held me fast, as if her very gaze was a trap, set to spring on who so ever fell under it. And indeed it was a trap.

'Good morning, Miss Beniot.' I greeted her as she glided into the study. 'Are you ready to get started on our first lesson this beautiful morning?'

A large yawn was emitted from Isabella as she plopped down, very un-lady like, into the chair before me and stared at me in a bored fashion.

'And what is this first lesson?' she asked, obviously not expecting much from me.

'I understand that you are quite fond of philosophy, as am I.' I answered, 'So, I felt that we would do well to base our new friendship on things that we both enjoy. I will provide a statement and you may respond with one of your own.'

A bit of amusement seemed to play across her face. My approach was new to her, not like the tutors before me, perhaps even inviting. I began.

'Life is but a moment, stolen from time, that it shall soon take back again.'

Isabella's eyes narrowed, intrigued, as she sat upright and spoke.

'The hand of death has its nails ripped away by moments of time, refusing to pass by.'

'Very good!' I complimented, applauding her statement, 'Very defiant! It seems that you have the fighting spirit of your father inside of you!'

'What I have, Mister Bell,' she responded, 'is my own spirit and it is a free one that has no such price as honor, pride, or earthly possessions. I know why you are here and I appreciate your trouble, I really do, but there is nothing that you can teach me here. I want to go out into the world and experience life, not waste my days away, locked away in the safety of this mansion, locked away from the world.'

'Isabella,' I said, seeing a chance to set foot on common ground with her, 'I have my own spirit as well, free of monetary compensation. My true reward comes from helping others, spreading my knowledge, forming bonds with kindred souls. I think you and I could have those bonds if you were to open your mind to me, but unless you accept the challenge to find out we will never know.'

'And what is this challenge, Mister Bell?' she asked, interest in my statement apparent.

'To allow me the chance to teach you, while you, in turn, teach me. To allow us both to grow. To show me who you really are, inside. There is so much to explore. All you have to do is agree.'

Isabella watched me intently, her eyes narrowing slightly, always glittering, assessing the world around her. A child-like smirk played across her angel's face. She nodded.

'Though my heart is already far from this place, strolling the streets of Paris, I accept your challenge, Mister Bell.' she said, her hand playing unconsciously along the spine of her small book, 'You are different from the others in the parade of idiots. Maybe you do have something to teach me after all.'

Chapter 18

"The following months seemed a blur. Isabella became an island to me, a bright shining star trapped inside a void of darkness. The Beniot brothers did not warm to me much and seemed concerned as Isabella and I became closer. My feeling grew stronger for her but I was sure to keep them hidden away, afraid of her reaction, should she learn the truth. I was afraid, also, of her father's response if he found that the man that he had trusted to tutor his beloved daughter had fallen in love with her. He kept a close eye on our progress through his sons, his wavering health often keeping him confined to his quarters. Isabella's studies went well, yet her father began having reservations about our time together, after all, none of the other tutors had lasted more than a few weeks, but he was pleased that her talk of Paris had ceased, at least for the time being.

Isabella and I had become fast friends, each of us feeling alone in this world and finding solace in each other. She was ambitious and had curious ways in which she saw the world which gave me cause to see myself in her. She was amazing."

"You loved her that deeply?" Miranda asked, shaking William from his recollected thoughts.

"From the very first moment that I saw her." he answered then continued his story.

"Perhaps it was the strained relationship with her father that helped kindle the kinship that I shared with her. Out of our friendship grew a great trust, yet I couldn't bring myself to tell her about the horrors of my youth and how my father still haunts my dreams, but she opened up to me about her mother and watching her as she grew ill and slowly died. She talked of how her father, a man that she thought was unbreakable, fell to pieces after her death, sealing off her mother's bedroom, the room that she had died in, and not allowing anyone to enter. She told me of slipping into that room a year after her mother's death and the bed that she died upon still holding her imprint in the sheets, as if she had just woken and left, leaving the bedding unmade. Isabella began visiting her mother's room often, in the darkest hours of night, unbeknownst to her father, brushing her hair with her mother's brush, letting her hair mingle with the strands left from the last time her mother had brushed her own hair, curling up on the floor with her mother's favorite red gown, trimmed in golden threads, so that she could recall her smell again. She discovered a box, hidden away in her mother's possessions. Upon opening it she found a journal filled with many years of stories, writings, and poetry, all penned by her mother's hand. This was the small book that was she kept constantly in her presence. She had taken the journal from the room and studied her mother's work, memorizing all of it over the years. She shared some of it with me as she grew more comfortable in our friendship. Her mother's writings were filled with dark verses, bleak and frightening, especially the ones that were penned as her health declined and death approached. I began to see a darkness in Isabella, a darkness grown from despair and loneliness, a darkness that was all too familiar to me. The fall gave way to winter, winter to spring, and as summer approached, we would argue those late spring days about our philosophies and politics, poetry and arts, sometimes late into the night, outside, walking the grounds of the plantation. Isabella found in me something that she had not from the other tutors, her brothers, or her even her father. Respect. In turn, Isabella held my views, my words, and above all, my feelings with high regard. Of course, I returned this to her. As her father became more aware of our deepening friendship that had formed outside of the professional boundary of student and teacher I could sense that I stood under strong scrutiny with him. His words to me on my duties concerning his daughter, all of those months ago, still held strong in my mind.

I had promised to follow his wishes, but with Isabella it was impossible not to be captivated by her. Fall was now nearing its end and I had passed the one year mark at the Beniot household. It was late in the evening. Isabella's father was feeling ill, suffering still from his unrelenting, chronic, cough and had retired for the night. She and I had taken our supper in the study, avoiding her brothers, as was a common practice. Isabella had sneaked a bottle of wine from the servants and she and I had indulged a bit too much, it seems. We made our way out of the house through one of the back entrances and into the maze like garden area which stretched out behind the mansion. The wine warmed our bodies, chasing away the nip in the night air. Distant lightning flickered and streaked across the sky like the angry claws of some forgotten god and the sound of rumbling thunder could be heard, as Isabella laughed and danced about.

Marble statues of angels stared out from confining undergrowth of vines, some cracked and broken from age, like lost ghosts waiting patiently for someone to free them of their earthly bindings. We walked through the twisting corridors with a determined, fast pace, our hair whipping about in the chilly breeze, Isabella's dress fluttering around her. We had walked these paths many times before, but tonight was different. As the storm drew closer our reactions both physically and mentally matched its swelling intensity. Our steps were furious, so was our laughter, and our conversation, which was originally on one of our favorite plays, but due to our wine overindulgence, had shifted to her father and brothers.

The wind howled as the first heavy, cold, drops of rain battered our skin. Isabella roared her defiance to the angry skies above.

'Do you know what it's like, God?!' she howled 'Do you?!'

I endured the whipping wind, my mouth hanging open at her questioning the creator. The bellowing currents of air blew through the trees around the plantation, producing a shriek like the souls of ten thousand dead moaning from within their graves, sending chills over my body.

'He holds me here in this place! In her place!' she screamed pointing towards the burial yard where her mother's body rests, tears now streaking her face. 'He tries to make me what she was! I am not his wife! I am his daughter, deserving of my own life away from this dreadful place, away from her memory that he imprisons me with! Every reprimand that is heaped upon me, in her comparison, slashes deep into my mother's memory, spilling more resentment upon my soul! My mother understood me!'

She threw her head back screaming at the angry sky again, 'Damn you! Why did you take her from me?'

I rushed forward as the cold rain fell, grabbing her head in my hands and turning her face to mine.

'Isabella...' I whispered.

'I tell you this, William,' she growled above the elements, a wildness in her tear filled eyes, 'he builds a ghost, enraged!'

I knew not if she spoke of God or her father.

'Isabella...' I whispered again, 'You are... We are drunk! We should return to the mansion!'

Isabella watched me through the sheets of rain. The wild look was still shining in her eyes and a strange smile crossed her pretty face.

'We stand in the shadows of an enchanted garden, hunters of sanity in a world gone mad.' She said, reciting lines from a favorite of her mother's poems.

She spun about, her arms extended, laughing as her tears mixed with the rain and fell across her pale cheeks. Her dress, heavy with the early November rain, clung to her, making clear the contours of her body. Suddenly she stopped her spinning and strode towards me.

'Isabella...' I muttered again.

She paused before me, watching me, rain drops dripping from her long lashes. The heart of the storm, it seemed, had found us. The earth shook beneath its onslaught, the wind and rain tearing at us, stinging our flesh. The lightning flashed in wicked streaks exploding against the far off countryside. During this, a calmness seemed to overtake Isabella, a calmness that she spread to me through her gaze. She reached out, taking me by the shoulders and drew close to me. Her soft skin pressed against my cheek as she whispered into my ear.

'Just as we struggle to overcome the evil inside of ourselves, invisible angels battle above us, unknown to us, for the fate of our Hell, and we each become another thorn in the crown of doom!'

I extended my arms, pushing her away.

'Isabella!' I shouted, 'Why must you always speak in these damned poetic riddles?!'

A look of shock, almost betrayal, befell her as she spoke, 'Here! Now! Cry your tears! For love lost! Dreams crushed! Any wrongs that torment your soul! Tonight, our tears mix with the tears of God himself! He can know your sorrow!'

'He already knows my sorrow!' I countered, a tinge of anger trailing my voice.

'And he can never know mine.' Isabella said quietly.

She lunged towards me and then her lips were on mine. Time stopped. Emotions overwhelmed me as her soft mouth pressed against me. Fear, shock, anger, and grief swirled together inside of me, crafting an excitement that I had never known. The sweet embrace lasted but a moment and she released me. We stood facing each other in the frigid down pour. I could see surprise, perhaps of the bravery of her own actions, etched into her face, as well as her fear of my rejection. She had the look of a scared little girl, not the over confident teen that I was in love with. She had entrusted me with her most kept secret, her vulnerability."

'Isabella.' I said her name again, not knowing what else to say. I smiled to her and she returned the smile in her usual charming and arrogant fashion, her weakness vanishing as quickly as it had appeared. We turned and made our way out of the garden to the mansion, not realizing that the moment that we had just shared would change everything.

We raced up the stone steps at the back of the manor towards the rear entrance. In the flashes of lightning of the passing storm, I noticed that the large door leading to the rear of the mansion stood open to the elements and that someone stood just inside the threshold.

'You had best get to your room, little sister,' boomed the voice of Brusion Beniot with a loudness that seemed to put it on a par with the rolling thunder outside. 'and change from your soaked garments before you catch your death of cold.'

Isabella, usually always spoiling for a confrontation with her brothers once she felt that their will was being imposed on her, found herself emotionally spent and surprising Brusion and me alike, nodded her head in agreement.

'Good evening, brother.' She spoke quietly through chattering teeth, as she nodded to Brusion and turned back to me. 'Good evening, Mister Bell.'

Isabella gathered the edges of her heavy, rain soaked dress and quickly made her way to the stairway that led to her room leaving Brusion and me with the strange silence that I had grown somewhat accustomed to around him and his brother. Faking a yawn, I placed a hand over my mouth. 'I, too, should retire for the evening. We have a long day of studies ahead of us tomorrow.' I said, trying to create my escape from Brusion's company.

I attempted to walk past the large man, but was suddenly in his stone like grip. He spun me about, slamming me against the mansion wall. My breath was pushed from my lungs from the forceful collision. I gasped for air as I felt the same inhuman grip clasping my throat and forcing my head back so that I stared up into his face. In the flickering lighting I could see the fury in Brusion's eyes. His hair and clothing were heavy with rain. A sick feeling overtook me as he spoke to me in a rasping whisper.

'I heard her screams.' he growled, 'I ventured into the garden to investigate. I heard everything. I saw everything.'

His voice grew louder as he tightened his already crushing grip. My eyes bulged under the pressure.

'You were to tutor her! We trusted in you! My father trusted in you! Now I hear my dear sister damning God himself while in a drunken stupor?! Blasphemous! And what do you do? Condone it with your lips upon hers! What have you taught her?!'

I could not speak within his grip. I truly thought it was to be my end there at the edge of the garden where I had just kissed the woman that I loved.

'My father only wishes for Isabella to be safe within these walls,' He spun me about, slamming me against another wall, expelling what breath I had left, 'Not safe in your arms! I could see your intentions months ago. You think you can seduce my sister and find your way into the riches that this family has to offer?! You fool!'

His body shook with rage as he grabbed my hair in one of his huge fists, pulling my head backwards.

'You are to pack your belongings this night, Mister Bell.' Brusion commanded, 'and you are to be gone from this plantation before my dear sister wakes. You will not seek council with my father and you will not say any farewells. You will depart as you arrived, unceremoniously. Is this understood?'

'Yes.' I squeaked as he relinquished his grip a bit, allowing me to answer.

'If you ever lay eyes upon my sister again, it will be I that teaches you a final lesson.' He warned. With his immense strength he tossed me, bodily, down the hallway leading from the room. I fell hard against the wooden floor, hitting my face. I lay there, dazed and gasping for breath, hearing Brusion's footsteps approach me, for what I took to be the killing blow. Mercifully, he passed me by and I pushed myself from the floor, struggling to stand.

'I will have a carriage brought around to take you back to New Orleans within the hour. Be ready.' he warned as he headed deeper into the vast house.

I walked unsteadily to my room, heartbroken, and started assembling my belongings. What would Isabella think of me? What would her brother's tell her? What would become of her? I fought back tears as I realized that I may never see this beautiful girl again. It took little time to prepare for my departure. I peered out the window of my bedroom at the distant storm, moving away from the Beniot house and toward New Orleans, ironically in the direction that I was soon to travel. Below I could see servants, awakened from their slumber, making their way to the stables to prepare my coach. How could I simply leave without saying my farewell to my Isabella? I couldn't bear her not knowing the truth.

My love for Isabella overshadowing my fear of her brother, I foolishly slipped from my room and keeping to the shadows, made my way to her bedroom. I slunk through the door and eased into her room like a thief, creeping to her bedside.

'Isabella!' I whispered, 'Isabella!'

I extended my arm up onto her bed, groping in the darkness, but my hand found only a warm place where her body had lain.

'I am here!' called Isabella's hushed voice from the far corner of her room.

Startled, I spun about and looked into the blackness.

'Isabella,' I said, my voice choked with emotion, 'I must leave... tonight.'

I took several steps forward, blindly, in the direction from which her voice came.

'Your brother, Brusion,....he saw us...saw everything that transpired in the garden.'

'I know.' came her reply, whispered close to my ear, unnerving me. 'Perhaps now you have tears that God does not know of yet?'

'What?!' I responded in disbelief, as I regained my composure, 'You knew?! How?!'

'I saw him,' she answered calmly, 'spying on us, following us through the manor halls and out into the garden. Everything that I said was because of his eavesdropping. Yes, he heard and saw everything. Our words. Our kiss.'

I stood in the darkness of her room, staring, dumbfounded, into the pitch black where Isabella hovered somewhere before me, unraveling her twisted web of manipulation.

'You orchestrated this...this madness?! For God's sake, why?!' I whispered loudly into the pitch black. 'I must leave here now, leave you!'

Her words broke through the dark room, halting my own.

'Why must this be about your loss?' she asked.

'Isabella,' I replied, 'Why would you do this to me? I thought we were friends.'

'I thought we were more.' She retaliated from the darkness, silencing me.

'I knew that when Brusion saw us kiss that he would react this way, send you away. I have my belongings packed, William, and I am ready to travel.' Isabella said, 'When you leave, I will go with you! We will be free to travel this world as we see fit! It shall belong to us! What great adventures we will have together! We can even travel to Paris!'

I was speechless, my mind wondering if this were some dream.

'William,' she said, softly, sweetly, 'I love you.'

I felt her warm breath on my ear, then her soft lips upon my neck and for a moment, I could not move.

'Isabella,' I stammered, as her rose petal smell filled my nostrils, 'I cannot!' I protested weakly.

'Yes, my love, you can.' she answered back, 'We can!'

Mustering all of my willpower, I turned away from the woman that I so desired, the woman whom had just professed her love for me and spoke, 'I cannot. You cannot. I will leave here in a few short moments, alone. I am sorry, Isabella, I came to say farewell.'

I darted from her room, confused, wanting nothing more than to fall into Isabella's arms and let my lifetime of pain and hurt drift away, but I couldn't. I had no means to care for her should we flee the Beniot plantation together and though a year had passed, I couldn't forget that I was surely still sought after for the death of my father.

Leaving her behind, though it may have seemed cruel and it may have broken my heart, was indeed what was in her best interests, after all, her father was not in good health and would not live forever. Perhaps then she would be free to travel where she wanted, far away from her controlling brothers.

I retreated to my room only long enough to gather my baggage. I lugged what I could carry to the main entrance of the mansion, shivering in my still wet clothes. This seemed a nightmare now, one that I watched from afar. I stepped out onto the porch, which was covered in the mighty storm's residue, dragging my bags behind me. The smell of the rain water on the stone walk and the stench of damp soil was carried on the cold breeze. These were to be my last memories of the Beniot house. These were my last few moments close to Isabella. Isabell, my friend, my love...my beautiful angel. I had failed her. I had failed her just as much as her father had by keeping her locked away, wasting her years, a prisoner in her own home, just as her mother had when she slipped, silently, away leaving a young girl lost and afraid. I, too, left her stranded, assigned to her fate within those manor halls.

What right did I have to make that decision for her, that she must stay at her home? Who was I to make that decision for her when, as a child, my very survival depended on me fleeing my own home.

I was no one to tell her this. I had no right. As my guilt mounted I could hear the rhythm of the horses' footfalls on the stone walk as the coach was brought around for me. The carriage lurched to a stop. The driver waited while I wasted no time in loading my belongings. I stepped up into the coach. Looking back, I could see the muscular forms of the Beniot brothers, Brusion and Jacob, peering down from one of the balconies overhead, observing my final moments at their home. Shuddering under their watchful eyes' I began the long ride back to New Orleans. I stared back at the plantation house as it drifted into the dismal Louisianan night, a lump in my throat and my heart breaking, already missing that annoying, wonderful, headstrong girl locked away within the walls of her father's castle. Lost in this void of sadness, I pulled my cloak about me and drifted off to sleep in the predawn gloom."

Chapter 19

"Mental exhaustion must have had a stronger grip on me than I had first realized. Throughout most of the day's nonstop jostling of the coach, I somehow managed to stay deep inside the numbing cocoon of sleep. Only at dusk, like some damned vampyre, did I stir. Sitting up I groggily looked around, recognizing the outskirts of New Orleans. The driver of the coach slowed the horses until they came to a stop. Confused, I leaned up and called to him.

'Sir?' I asked, 'Is something the matter? Why have we stopped?'

The driver turned to face me, pulling open the heavy cloak and removing the brimmed hat, revealing the beautiful, smiling face of Isabella Beniot.

'Our adventure begins here, my love!' she chirped with excitement, tears of happiness in her eyes.

'Isabella!' I yelled, my chest swelling with joy, bewildered by her unexpected surprise.

'What are you doing?' I questioned in disbelief, 'Your father...'

'My father is now just a fleeting memory of my past.' She said as she hopped into my lap, 'And, you, Mister Bell, are my future!'

Her mouth was on mine again, her smell engulfing me. My eyes closed, lost in her touch. Her tongue teased my lips and I felt as if I were on fire. As the kiss ended we embraced, unafraid, staring out into the dying sunset on the blood red horizon, tears of joy and hope being blinked away. Darkness fell and we continued on into New Orleans. By then her brothers were surely on their way to find her. I cannot express the feeling that overtook me that evening. I was so happy to have Isabella with me, so excited about the life that we could build together if we could just slip quietly away. I was happy that she was happy. I heard laughter from her, pure blissful laughter that was so contagious that I laughed hysterically along with her. But beneath this veil of joy I was selfish. In my heart I knew that what we were about to undertake was doomed. I had very limited funds and Isabella's brothers, both soldiers, were hunters and trackers. They had near limitless resources at their disposal. The Beniot family was well known in this area and if we were to stay in New Orleans we would be found, it was just a matter of time. I would be arrested and possibly face execution if they were to trace my past back to New York and Isabella would be brought back to the Beniot plantation to be locked away again. Our only hope was to flee, but Isabella had other ideas. She had brought enough funds to ensure our passage to France and we found the ship was set to sail within two days time. She had planned every aspect.

'How long have you been scheming this, your escape?' I asked her. She smiled her undeniable smile.

'Since I fell in love with you.' she replied, leaving me smiling like a love struck fool.

'And how shall we survive in Paris?' I asked Isabella, 'What if we starve? Are you prepared to become a beggar on the streets, just to escape your family?'

Isabella looked at me in silence, an unnatural seriousness falling across her pretty face.

'I would beg, as long as I am with you,' she said, 'as I beg you now. Show me this world.'

Never had I felt such a connection with another living soul, not even my mother. She was undeniable to me. What did I have in this world now? Nothing, except this young woman who sat beside me. I had Isabella, now and forever.

'You will go to Paris with me?' she asked, sheepishly, like a child asking a question but fearing the answer.

I lowered my eyes from hers, swallowed hard and answered, 'Yes, we shall go to Paris.'

'Yes?' Isabella exclaimed, her squeals of delight echoing throughout the streets of the darkening city, drawing more attention than I wished, as she threw her arms about my neck, 'We are going to Paris!'

I couldn't help but laugh at her excitement.

'Thank you, William!' she cried, 'Thank you!'

I smiled at the joy that my words brought to her, telling a story of someone who had been denied too much thus far in life.

Isabella looked at me, a devilish smirk crossing spreading across her face.

'I, also, would not concern myself much about starving once we reach Paris. You see, I liberated a bit of my inheritance as a bon voyage gift from my father.' She said, grinning.

'You little sneak!' I said, grinning at her mischievousness. The very real threat of her brothers on our trail crept into my thoughts, chasing away the excitement of the moment.

'Isabella, if we are to avoid capture by your brothers while we wait for our ship to sail, we must find a place to hide! Now!' I said.

We both knew that her brothers would be on their way and that they would be moving much faster than our carriage had. They may have been just a couple of hours behind us by then. We deserted the buggy and horse a few blocks from the port and dragged our baggage through the streets to a small alehouse with rooms available for rent located near where our ship would depart. Isabella kept her heavy coat buttoned tight and the brimmed hat upon her head pulled down low to conceal her identity as we entered the dim tavern. We made our way through the noisy crowd and the tobacco smoke to the bar, where the barkeep stood pouring rum and ale for his patrons. There was all manner of riff-raff about the place. Scantily clad women hung on drunken men, card games were being bet on in the corners. Raucous laughter and singing seemed to come from all directions at once.

'Sir,' I shouted over the uproarious crowd, 'I need a room for me and my...'

'Brother.' Isabella said, ending my awkward silence.

I looked back to Isabella, suppressing my amusement. The rotund bald man looked quizzically from me to Isabella in her disguise.

'Brother, eh?' he asked.

Keeping her face lowered, Isabella pushed several silver coins across the top of the bar to which the bald man smiled. He pocketed the coins and reached under the bar, producing a worn brass key. He handed it to me and motioned towards a set of stairs near the rear of the bar.

'Up the stairs, third door down the hall.' He grumbled.

I turned back to Isabella and spoke, Come, Nicholas, we have had a long journey and I am tired.'

I could see her contagious smile from beneath the shadows of her hat brim. 'Yes, brother.' She mocked in a feigned deep voice which nearly caused me to burst with laughter, as she followed me through the mass of people toward the stairs. We made our way up to our room and placed our belongings in a corner. The room was small with meager furnishings; a small one person bed, one chair and a tiny table. There was one window in the room overlooking the port, allowing the muddy smell of the Mississippi River to be carried in on the cool breeze. I walked to the window and admired the view of the moon reflecting off of the waters and the fascinating steam boat as it propelled its way up the river. Isabella was behind me, her arms encircling me and her head resting on my shoulder.

'We are really doing this, aren't we?' she asked.

I turned to face her, my arms holding her in my embrace. 'Yes, we are.'

Isabella flashed another of her mischievous smiles.

'You lived here in New Orleans, yes?' she asked.

'Yes, but only for a short while before I came to your home.' I answered.

'I've only been here once, as a little girl. From what I remember it was like another world. Can we go out and see a bit of the city? The Saint

Louis Cathedral, perhaps? Just a taste of France to show me what the true country has in store for us?'

She must have seen the worried look upon my face. She leaned forward and kissed me gently.

'I'll wear my coat and hat!' she grinned.

I could not deny her. I dressed with my long cloak pulled around me which felt good as the chilly night air filled our room. She donned her coat and hat as I closed the window and we left our room, once more wading through the sea of humanity to the bar where we indulged in a few glasses of wine. Our drinks finished, we pushed our way out onto the streets and began exploring the city. We followed the streets that I knew from the short time that I was in the city. Isabella marveled at the architecture of the buildings and babbled on about how things would be in Paris. Soon we were traveling down Rue de la Levée towards the Place d'Armas and the cathedral.

'You know,' Isabella spoke, her words slightly slurred from the powerful drink that we had taken, 'the Place d'Armas was designed after the Place des Vosges in Paris! We will have to go there when we arrive in France to see how closely they resemble each other!'

'You say that you have only been here, to New Orleans once before, how do you know such things?' I asked.

'My mother was from Paris and moved to New Orleans as a little girl,' she answered, pulling her mother's journal from the pocket of her coat and holding it with both hands over her heart. 'She would tell me stories of the wonders here and abroad. She promised that she would take me to Paris one day and show me, first hand, the fantastic splendors of which she spoke. Death, however, took her first.'

Now it became clear to me why Paris pulled so strongly at her heartstrings.

'William!' she gasped, 'Look at it! It's magnificent!'

We stood before the impressive St. Louis cathedral, its two towers stretching high above us, flanking the main church. Some construction seemed underway upon the roof, no doubt building upon the structure's grandeur.

'Yes,' I replied nonchalantly, 'I suppose it is.'

Isabell turned with her mouth open in mock offense, 'How dare you act as if this is not impressive! As if you see such as this on a daily affair!'

We both fell into laughter and continued on our exploration of the city and until the chill of the deepening night forced us to return to our room at the inn. We entered the alehouse in the wee hours of the morning. The bar was still thick with people to whom time had no meaning. Exhaustion had set upon both Isabella and me as we made our way up the stairs to our room, oblivious to the strange looks from the bar keeper. We were loud with laughter and discussion as we walked down the hall to our room. I fumbled with the key a bit before opening the door and then we entered our room. The candles in our room had been extinguished. Strange, I thought, as I had closed the window before we left earlier. I stepped back into the hallway and retrieved a candle from one of the sconces. I returned to our room to light our own and stepping through the doorway, in the soft, yellow, glow of my candle light I saw that we had already been found by Jacob Beniot. His brawny back was turned to me with Isabella, firmly, in his grips. With one swift backhanded slap she was sent sprawling across the room, collapsing against the wall.

'How dare you, girl?!' Jacob screamed, 'Putting our father through such Hell as this?!'

He seemed oblivious or possibly unconcerned with me as he stalked towards his sister.

'Brusion and I have been riding since we found you missing at sunrise! At first we thought you were taken against your will, but the "goodbye" note that you left for our father? We found it first. He will never know of what you have done. We will place all of the blame on Bell. You will gather your things now and return home with us.'

Isabella looked up from the floor, her hand touching her swollen lip.

'No!' she hissed back, 'I will not go back to that prison! Not with you! Not with anyone!'

'How could you be so cruel, sister?' he asked as he moved closer to her. 'Have you lost all of your senses?'

'No, you muscle bound fool!' she yelled, 'I have come to my senses!'

Jacob pulled his sister from the floor by the heavy coat that she still wore and pushed her back against the wall.

'You will come back with us, now!' He spat.

Isabella struggled in his grasp. I could see the thin trickle of blood from her nose and upper lip as she looked up at her brother, defenselessly. I dropped the candle and darted across the dark room, throwing myself upon Jacob, flailing at him wildly, attempting to protect Isabella. I was upon his back, my arms clasped tightly around his neck. I felt his powerful body moving around with ease beneath my weight.

'This is a family affair, Bell!' he roared as he flipped me over his shoulder, sending my smashing to the floor on the back of my neck. I must have blacked out for a moment as I remember the pressure from his fists colliding with my face, but realized no pain.

His voice penetrated the fog of the assault.

'You should have taken your leave when you had the chance, you fool!' his words echoed from far away.

I could hear Isabella's screams from across the room. My vision cleared slowly and I could make out Jacob holding me to the ground with his hand at my throat, looking down at me. My life was slowly being squeezed from my body by Jacob, something that I suspect he had desired to do since our first meeting a year ago.

Isabella, bless her and her stubbornness, her courage! She slid the belt from her heavy coat and threw it over her brother's head. She placed all of her weight against his lower back and pulled the belt, securing it around his thick neck. A look of surprise came across Jacob's face, which quickly turned to panic, as he came to the realization that it was now he that was struggling for breath. A snarl of anger on her face, Isabella licked the blood from her lips as she tightened her grip and cursed her brother. Releasing his hold on me, Jacob tried working his fingers in between the belt and his throat. I could see the look of grim determination on Isabella's face. This was years of pent up frustrations being avalanched down upon her well deserving victim.

'Run, William.' She said to me calmly, a smirk of satisfaction on her face. 'Run!' she said louder, in an assertive manner, 'I'll be along in a few moments, once I finish with these "family affairs".'

Jacob's face was turning a deep shade of purple as he continued to struggle beneath his sister's weight and leverage, but Isabella held fast empowered by a lifetime of anger, tightening her grip to what must have seemed to Jacob to be superhuman levels. I scrambled to my feet and staggered to the door.

'Isabella!' I pleaded, 'You are killing him!'

Even in the shadows I could see her impish smile, revealing her realized power over her brother. She held his life in her hands. Poor, defenseless, Isabella. If only her father could see her now. If only he could see his son that he was so proud of, at the mercy of his little girl.

'Now, love,' she grunted as she strained to pull yet harder on the belt that looped around her brother's neck, 'if I were to kill this oaf, and believe me my brother, I can, it would not make his existence nearly as miserable as letting him live, knowing that he was bested by his helpless, weak, little sister; the little sister who refuses to follow the orders of our father, the defenseless little girl that holds something as precious as the gift of his very life in her hands. Or should I finish him and end his embarrassment?'

She looked down to Jacob, gritting her teeth, 'Go, now, William, while I make my decision.'

Jacob's mouth was open wide, his eyes straining, threatening to pop from their sockets, as I turned and ran from the room, past several guests who had left the confines of their own quarters to see what the commotion was. Still groggy from my beating, I used the wall to help me navigate down the stairs and across the barroom, stumbling out into the sobering cold of the New Orleans streets.

A few moments later, though it seemed like an eternity as I waited, Isabella came sprinting from the inn carrying what bags she could, and joined me in the street where I stood gathering my senses. Through my swollen eye, I looked at my bruised Isabella.

'Isabella,' I said questioningly, fear, undoubtedly in my voice, 'Where is your brother? Where is Jacob? Did you...'

'Kill him?' she interrupted, 'No.'

I swear that I detected a bit of disappointment in her words as she spoke, 'I choked him until he stopped struggling, but when I released the belt, he gasped for air.'

‘We must go!’ I exclaimed as I grabbed her by her hand, ‘before the local authorities or your other damned brother shows up! Surely he is not far away!’

Isabella nodded in agreement. Without looking back and with just the clothes that we had on and what belongings were in the bags that she had managed to grab, we vanished into the dark streets of New Orleans”.

Chapter 20

"The next day we hid away in the streets of the city, getting lost amongst the vagabonds, avoiding her brothers. We watched from afar as people loaded aboard the ship that was to take us across the ocean to France. We spotted both Brusion and Jacob moving among the passengers as they boarded, standing out like giants, searching for us. The ship sailed away that day, carrying the hopes and dreams of Isabella Beniot and myself with it. We could not stay in the open streets of New Orleans any longer as the hunt for us continued. It was only a matter of time before we would be found if we were to do so. Our only choice was to flee from the city and hide in the surrounding countryside until we could secure our passage on another ship that was due to leave in a weeks time.

This was a near hopeless quest that was set before us. We knew that her father would never give up, that her brothers, lap dogs that they were, would continue the hunt us for as long as the old man willed. They would not stop until Isabella was dragged, kicking and screaming if need be, back to the Beniot plantation where she would be imprisoned there under her father's watchful eye.

   We were now fugitives, something that I was somewhat familiar with. Warm beds to chase away the chill of the night were a thing of the past. This was all-together new for Isabella, who had only known the safety and comfort of her families' mansion. Gone were the spoiled lives that we both had become accustomed to on the plantation. We had empty bellies but our hearts were full of dreams. Outside of the city we found shelter beneath an old bridge that crossed a shallow creek, which trailed off to eventually run into the Mississippi river. It was there, beneath the stars, as the cold night fell on us, that we held each other tight to keep warm. It was there that Isabella became my lover for the first time. It was there that I knew that I never wanted to be without her. We had each other and that was enough to push the ghost of our past away. I rarely thought of my dead father anymore, the hunched over old demon, but sometimes in my sleep I could still see him standing and staring out of his upstairs window, still hating me. Now though, if I were to awaken in terror, Isabella would be there to hold me in her arms and push the awful thoughts of those nightmares far away. As that night passed, we held each other closer, discussing our future together. How wonderful that sounded, a future with a family, far from New York and far from the Beniot plantation. A new start, a new home awaited us in a foreign land. A home that would one day be filled with the laughter of our children. Isabella and I were planning our life together, while lingering under that bridge. For two more days and nights we camped there, hiding away under the bridge when travelers crossed, braving the cold nights in each other's arms, talking away the long days with the plans for our future. Isabella would read to me some of the dark passages from her mother's journal, confusing things that I had never heard and things that I didn't fully understand, though to her the writings were clear and meaningful. My love for her doubled during those precious days, those long hours.

We woke early on the third morning to ominous clouds swirling in the grey sky. The wind blew with a chilling bite, coming off of the cold water of the creek. Isabella did not look well this morning. She seemed more pale than usual and her skin burned with fever. We had eaten our last bits of food the day before and the exposure to the elements over the past few days had taken a toll on us both. I knew that we had to find shelter, more than just this bridge. With less than a week left until the next ship to Paris was set to depart, I made the decision that we should head back to New Orleans and find a warm place for her to rest for the remainder of our time there.

Isabella had developed a terrible cough, reminding me very much of her father's. Her entire body shook when the fits overtook her. Before mid-day, her fever had risen and the coughing fits had progressed to the point that she would collapse from exhaustion and lack of breath. By the time we had reached the Port area a light drizzle of cold rain had begun to fall upon the city and the sun had started to set. Being mindful of her brothers possibly still lying in wait, I led Isabella through the back alleys to the burned out building that I called home when I first came to New Orleans, hoping that I remembered the way and praying that it had not been torn down.

My memory served us well and I led us straight to it. Part of the structure near the front had collapsed since I had last been there, but the building yet stood! I had to move charred lumber and debris out of the way so that we could gain access inside. I supported Isabella's weight as we maneuvered through the ruined building, dodging the leaking ceilings and fallen beams, until we reached the small room that had been my shelter all those months ago. I eased Isabella onto the old abandoned straw bed that I has slept on and covered her with my cloak to try to keep her warm. I crawled into the bed with her and cradled her head as she shivered, hoping my body heat would help to keep her warm, as she drifted off to sleep. I held her throughout her fitful sleep all that long night. Several times, she called out for me and several times, she called out for her mother.

The days passed and Isabella's sickness worsened as did the cold rain, which seemed endless, as it fell down upon the city."

Chapter 21

"I left Isabella in our make shift shelter and braved the cold streets to purchase some bread and dried meat for her. The intensity of this late fall storm had caught the city unprepared and the streets were mostly deserted. Though the rain had stopped falling a day before, the temperatures had not risen at all. The cold and dreary weather had kept most people in their homes or within the warmth of one of the many taverns about. I looked over my shoulder constantly, fearing that the Beniot brothers would show up at any moment to extract their revenge for stealing away their beloved sister. I hoped that they had moved on, searching elsewhere. We only needed one more day.

After procuring the food, I hastily returned to my love. When I made it back to her side, she was shivering violently and her horrible cough was producing traces of blood upon her lips, reminding me at once of the terrible illness that her father bore, which I figured to be slowly killing him. I looked into Isabella's pale face, her cheekbones even more prominent now, from lost weight from lack of nourishment. I placed my hand upon her forehead and she grasped my hand. Her head burned with the fever yet her hand was deathly cold, the icy grip of coming death.

I swallowed hard, blinking back my tears of concern, trying hard to hide my fears.

'Isabella,' I said, my voice choking, 'I've brought you food, you must eat to regain your strength.'

Isabella, empathic to my feelings, forced a smile.

'I'm not dying, you emotional twit.' She said weakly as her words trailed into another wracking cough.

'Isabella!' I exclaimed in alarm as I poured water that I had collected into a small glass that was left when the building was deserted.

'Here,' I said, putting the glass to her lips, 'drink.'

Isabella sipped a small amount then pushed the water away. I smiled to her as she eased back onto the bed, her breathing labored and raspy.

'You are looking much better today, Miss Beniot.' I lied to her, attempting to reassure her. 'By the time we make landfall in France, you must be rid of these ailments so that we can visit all of the places that you have told me of!'

'I will be fine, my love.' She wheezed, knowing that I was a horrible liar and what my words were intended to do.

I pulled the covers tight around her shivering body. I knew then if she didn't improve quickly that she may very well die here in this abandoned building. These thoughts were more than I could take. Isabella had already drifted back off to sleep so I sat there watching her sleep, staring at her beauty, which I feared was fading from this world. I listened to her ragged breathing, each breath an effort, each breath, breaking my heart. How could we have gotten so close to our hearts' desires, only to have them taken away again? I thought of our time on the plantation, our hours of constant discussion and bickering, our laughter and tears that we had shed. I could not bear her loss.

It was during these quite hours of reflection that I had to make a choice. If we stayed here, waiting on this ship to whisk us away to Paris, Isabella would die. Even if we were to make it aboard the ship she was much too weak to make such a long journey. She needed shelter, food, medication, things that I could not provide her here in this city, a city that we were being hunted in. Her survival meant that she must return home to her father.

I never left her side that night, going over in my mind how I would break this heartbreaking news to her. She stirred in her sleep, mumbling, shifting violently. I placed a hand gently on her shoulder to rouse her.

'Isabella?' I whispered, 'Isabella, wake up, dear. You are having a bad dream.'

Isabella's eyes flickered open in bewilderment.

'You were dreaming.' I repeated as I brushed her dark hair from her eyes.

She looked at me through heavy eyelids.

'It was so strange,' she said, 'so horrible. There were the souls of murdered children and they were collecting in great masses in the afterlife, awaiting their moment to revisit this world and deliver sentences to their murderers.'

I shook my head, 'No, my dear, just a dream. Your fever is very high and causing you these strange ideas.'

I gently stroked her hair and grew quite, unsure of how to continue, but time was something that I feared that Isabella didn't have much of.

'Isabella,' I said with a long pause before I found the nerve to continue, 'we must go back.'

I dropped my gaze, ashamed to look her in her eyes.

'Back to where?' Isabella asked weakly.

It took me a moment to summon the courage to answer her question.

'Back to your home, back to the plantation, back to your father, where you can recover from this illness.' I said bluntly, my voice cracking with emotion.

'What?!' she said, using her weakened arms to push herself up in the bed, 'What did you say?!'

'Isabella,' I reasoned, 'You are very sick. If we stay out here, you will die. You are in no shape to make the journey to Paris.'

'And if you force me back to that damned place, I will die!' she yelled, strength seeming to return to her body, fueled by her anger. 'By my own hand if need be!'

Isabella sprang from the bed, unsteadily to her feet. Frustration and outrage coursed through her frail body, rejuvenating her.

'You bastard!' she hissed as she staggered towards the doorway that led out into the ruined part of the building.

'Isabella, please!' I pleaded as I followed closely behind her, 'Please lay back down!'

'I have risked everything for you, William!' she yelled from ahead of me, spinning around to glare at me with a hatred that was usually reserved for her brothers.

Her words lit a fire in me as she turned and stormed through the ruined building towards the street.

'Tell me!' I yelled after her as I stayed upon her heels, 'Tell me of your sacrifices so that I may give you the attention and pity that you so secretly crave!'

I stopped for a moment, astonished at my outburst. These could have been words that I would speak to my own reflection and I was directing them at Isabella.

'What have you sacrificed, Isabella?' I continued, 'I have lost everything because of your little ploy in the garden! My career here is over! I have no home! I have nothing!'

Isabella stopped, now standing in the middle of the wet street.

'So I am nothing?' she asked me as I emerged out of the building.

'That is not what I meant!' I said, following her into the road, 'You are all that I have left in this world and I can't watch you die out in these streets like some damned animal because of your pride!'

My cheeks burned with the blood rushing to them and my heart raced as my pent up frustration eclipsed Isabella's own. Not to be out done, Isabella's teeth gritted in near uncontrolled fury. She approached me and lashed out, a mistake of actions that would change everything.

Her hand struck my face, violently turning my head to the side, staggering me. A great ringing in my ears ushered reality away from me. I do not know if it was the shock of the woman that I loved raising her hand against me or the built up rage from my past, but when I turned back to my attacker Isabella was not who stood before me.

The stinging pain of my face sent me tumbling into buried events of my past, of being scorned most of my life. Before me stood the sneering visage of my father.

An animalistic rage overtook me and I hurled myself into the old man, his white hair blowing, in wisps about his balding head and his usual expression of disgust on his face. Both of my hands wrapped around his throat, my speed knocking him onto his back in the street, my body crashing down on top of him. I looked into his eyes as my arms stiffened and all of my weight was placed on his throat. There was no fear in the old bastard's eyes, only hate, as he looked up at me. Then he began to laugh. I sat upon him, squeezing his life from him and he only laughed at me, mocked me!

'Stop laughing at me!' I screamed into his face, my voice echoing through the dark empty streets. I relinquished my death grip from his throat and started raining down my fists upon the old devil. Again and again I struck him, repaying every bruise from every beating that I had ever suffered at his hands. The laughter slowly faded and as I looked into his face, covered in the warm, steaming, crimson of his own blood, I finally saw emotion. I saw fear.

'William!' the devil gargled through bloody lips, 'Please stop! I love you!'

'I Love you!' the words hung in my ears. Tears poured down my face, spurred on by these heightened emotions. Blinking them away, the blurred image of my father's bloody and beaten face changed. No longer was it the image of the man that had tortured me throughout my childhood. I sat atop the chest of Isabella Beniot, my hands covered in her blood, her face a swollen mess, mumbling to me in a barely audible voice, 'I love you.'

I fell to the street beside her.

'No!' I screamed in disbelief, my heart breaking, 'This could not have happened!'

I pulled Isabella to me, cradling her head against my heart, and wept. How could this have happened? My father, now long dead, had almost taken Isabella from me! I carefully picked her up from the street and carried her back into the shelter of the empty building. I gently placed her on the bed and wetting bits of old cloth that we had used as make shift blankets, I began to cleanse the dried blood from her matted hair and her beaten face. I wept the entire time as she lay there, lifeless.

'How could I have done this?' I sobbed aloud as I wrapped Isabella's unconscious body in my cloak to keep her warm. I curled beside her on the small straw bed, pulling her close, my face buried in her hair, smelling the faint smell of rose petals over the dirt and grim of the street that we had been living in. My sweet Isabella. I held fast to the only thing that mattered in this world to me now, as she slowly slipped through my grasp. I cried myself to sleep, praying that when I woke that this nightmare had never happened, that I would wake to Isabella at my side, beautiful and healthy, playfully kissing my face, but the nightmare was just beginning. I drifted into troubled dreams, visions, if you will.

At first there seemed to be a wave of darkness cascading towards me, swallowing me completely, extinguishing all hope, just to prove its authority. I was powerless in its current, a lost ship in an angry sea of hate and pain. Then the visions began to take form. There, on the docks of the port where our ship was to sail for France, stood Isabella, her face unblemished and in seemingly perfect health. Standing beside her was the bloody faced figure of my father, his features swollen from the earlier beating. A small boy was standing close by watching the events unfold. There seemed to be a distant feeling of sorrow and pain hovering about the child as he looked towards me. Our eyes made contact and I knew, right away, that I was staring at my own soul.

My point of view suddenly shifted. I was overcome with the grief and sorrow of the boy. I stared upon the manifestation of love and hate, Isabella and my father, from the boy's point of view, from the depths of my own soul. I had no physical control. In a sense, I was as much imprisoned within myself as I am within this cell, helpless to do anything but watch as my father grabbed Isabella and hurled her off of the docks to the river below. Inside my head I screamed, loud enough I would have thought, to wake me from the vision, yet all it seemed to do was free me from the prison of my soul's perspective.

I drifted away, bodiless, from the boy. I could see Isabella's body, in the late stages of decay, caught in the Mississippi's current's far below. The image of my father was now approaching the still form of the little boy, standing lost in his own pain and suffering. My father dropped down onto his knees before the boy and seemed to regard him for a few moments. He then leaned forward, his mouth gaping open wide, and sank his teeth into the boy's throat, devouring him without resistance, swallowing him, swallowing my soul.

I felt that I was at the brink of insanity. I struggled with all that I had seen in this horror world. I turned away from this soul cannibal and back to the river where the corpse of Isabella Beniot seemed to come alive and drag itself out of its watery grave. I heard a scream, the boy, my soul's? Another's? I am not sure. I was cast away from this hell, back to reality, but I had no idea just how thin the seams between the two worlds really were.

I sat up, startled, sweat covering my body in my twisted, wet, clothing. After a moment of heavy breathing that I held no control over, I noticed that I was alone. Through the cracks in the ceiling overhead, I could see the sky showing the earliest signs of light. I looked about the room, searching for Isabella.

'Isabella?' I called, 'Isabella?!'

I rose upon weak knees and quickly made my way out to the street calling her.

'Isabella?!' I yelled. With the vison fresh on my mind I started running towards the port. 'Isabella?!' I screamed.

As I approached the river, my stomach was twisting in knots. I felt as if I were going to vomit as I drew closer to the dock and the places began matching up with the locations in my dream. I stepped upon the same spot as the boy stood in my vision. With all of the willpower that I could muster, I inched forward toward the dock.

'It was just a dream!' I whispered to myself, 'Just a horrible, horrible dream!'

I tried to quicken my pace. My heart fell to my stomach and my legs refused to work any longer. There, on the end of the dock, was my cloak that I had wrapped about Isabella to keep her warm. I dropped to my knees and crawled towards the familiar garment as it blew gently in the cold wind. Taking the heavy fabric in my hands, I found the journal of Lida Beniot hidden beneath it. I picked up the small book, Isabella's prized possession, and forced myself to the lip of the dock and looked down to the dark river below.

There was my Isabella, her body at the river's edge, floating face down in the cold waters a short distance from the ship that was to be our escape, just as in my accursed vision. She was dead. My Isabella was dead!"

Tears poured down William Bell's face as he recounted his story.

"But how was this possible?" he continued, "Dreams cannot kill, but my Isabella was dead. My love was dead. Our dreams, the plans that we had made just days earlier had died as well in the mud and murk of the cold Mississippi River. I turned and fled from Isabella and the river, spurred on by the paranoia of my vision, the thought of her corpse clawing its way back up the muddy bank to me. I ran, crying, hysterical, until I could not run any longer.

'Had she fallen into the water? Had she jumped?' these questions swirled around in my mind, which was numb with shock. Ultimately I would be accused of Isabella's death. I fled back to that old bridge that we had taken shelter under, where we had made love for the first time. I lay under that bridge for days trying to wish away the nightmare that my life had become, reading the pages of her mother's journal so that my mind would hear Isabella's sweet voice in my head, mourning my lost lover, but the farther I delved into that book, beyond the poetry, I discovered that there was something else. Deeper within those pages were strange symbols and things that I do not understand, frightful drawings and words that I am unable to pronounce all penned by the same hand that wrote the dark poems. These pages Isabella never spoke of. I read them over and over, each time feeling closer to her, as if she were with me, just a breath away. I eventually dragged myself out from under that bridge and I've been running ever since. The visions have continued, more frequently, more bizarre, each showing a grizzly prophecy destined to come to pass. The visions led me here, where I attempted to save those children, but she arrived before I could stop her."

"Isabella?" Miranda asked, her voice quivering as shew wiped away tears shed for William Bell's heartbreaking story.

"Isabella." he stated, his head dropping, "I know that you may think that I am mad, but I swear to you that Isabella Beniot is somewhere in this town, whispering to me at night, even in death, tormenting me for what I did to her. I tell you that I saw her the night that the children were murdered, watching from the upper windows of that hill top church as I was led back to the jail by your father. She teases me with the blood of innocents that I can never save."

The sun was now creeping towards the horizon and the last of the day's light covered the town in an orange glow. William studied the pretty young girl that stood in the shadows of the alley composing herself, obviously troubled after hearing his dreadful tale. This was to be his last sunset, his last night. If Isabella wished to hound him further she would soon have to cross through death's door again. She would have to follow him to Hell.

"You play the harp beautifully, Miranda." William said, smiling through the bars, "I would be indebted to you if you would play for me tonight, so that perhaps my final dreams are not of the terror and pain of this accursed sound that pillages my mind, but of beauty and peace, something that has long been denied me."

The girl smiled back to William, but before she could answer the gathering crowd in front of the jail began yelling and screaming. Something was happening.

"Go, Miranda! Quickly! Before you are discovered!" he whispered loudly to the sheriff's daughter. Miranda pulled her scarf around her head as she turned to flee the alley.

"And thank you!" he continued. She bolted down the alley and out into one of the town's small roads, vanishing from his sight.

Chapter 22

William turned away from the window and walked to center of his cell. There was a great commotion beyond the door, in the front room of the jail. Seconds later the door opened and two guards strode in followed by Sheriff Winston and Brusion Beniot, a cold smirk of satisfaction on his face. Behind the group, his steps a bit slower than the others, was a short, slender man with dark hair and a beard. His clothes were worn and dirty from his journey home and he seemed at the point of exhaustion. The small man moved past the guards to stand in front of the cell.

"This is him?" he stammered, "The one that killed my babies?!"

His voice became a roar as he lunged forward, grasping wildly through the bars at William Bell, who stood safely out of reach.

"You killed my babies!" he sobbed "They were all that I had left!"

Landon Taylor's knees buckled as he collapsed to the floor, his head resting against the cell bars, as he mourned.

"What threat did they pose to you?" he moaned, "What did you gain?"

William stood silent, gathering his nerves.

"Sir," he spoke softly, his voice full with pity and regret, "I did not kill your children. I swear to you, I did not."

"He may not have done the killing, but he is a part of it. The murder weapon was found among his belongings on his horse which was also found on your farm that night, Landon." Sheriff Winston said, stepping forward to place a hand on the emotionally distraught father.

"The evidence is overwhelming." the sheriff continued, "There is another involved, a woman, but though we have searched the town and the surrounding country we have found no sign of her. I am certain that she has moved on by now. The Lord will deal with her in his own time, I just pray that it is before she can kill again, but this one... his days of evil have come to an end. He and his companion have left a trail of death behind them for some time now. Come morning his part in this murderous binge will have come to an end."

Nathanial Winston looked up at William Bell through the bars.

"In mere hours, you will die." he said flatly.

The two guards reached down and grasped the grieving man beneath his arms and helped him to his feet. The sheriff turned and followed the father of the murdered children as he was led from the room. Brusion, however, lagged behind. He watched William as a predator would its prey. A smile played across his face.

"I'll cut your head from your body, Bell." he said, "I'll take it back to my father, so that he may enjoy firing his pistols into your face and when he tires of that I'll gather your remains and place them in his piss pot so that he may piss upon your skull for the rest of his days."

"If you had but left us alone, Isabella and I would be happily in Paris now, but no, you had to hound us, chase us. You, your brother, and father denied her any chance of happiness, content to keep a beautiful young woman locked away from the world. Why, Brusion?" William asked, bluntly.

"Because it was what my father wanted, what was best for my family." Brusion said coldly.

"But what about what was best for Isabella?!" William yelled.

"I do not have to explain my family's actions to the likes of you, murderer." Brusion replied.

"Murderer?! You and your family drove Isabella to her death, you bastard!" William said, his voice quivering with anger "You could have let us go. I could have made her happy, but no, you had to chase us down on your father's orders, didn't you? To attempt to drag her back to the plantation to be treated like a possession instead of the young woman that she was. Now she is still gone. Would it not have been better for her to live out her life in happiness instead going to her grave so young?"

"You put her there, you devil!" Brusion spat, "You alone."

"No, Brusion, you did." Bell said," You and your father drove her to it. He will not live forever. What will become of you then, Brusion? What will become of the sheep when the shepherd is no more? You will be lost, Brusion. Lost like sheep."

Brusion's smile turned to serious snarl. Through gritted teeth, he spoke, "It doesn't matter if the sheep are lost, once the wolf is dead."

Brusion turned and walked from the room, slamming the door behind him. Darkness engulfed William for a time as he sat against the cell wall, wishing that this was all over. After a while, the distant, distinct sound of Miranda's harp playing floated in on the evening breeze, lulling him into his final night of sleep.

Chapter 23

Darkness. Oblivion. Voices, muffled and distorted. Where was he? Bars? He was still in his cell. The roaring in his ears amplified the pounding inside his skull. Was it time for him to die yet, he wondered? William sat up from the straw covered floor. His bones ached and his muscles screamed. As he rubbed his eyes he became aware of another person standing inside his cell with him. Startled, William pushed away from his unknown visitor.

"Who's there?" he called out to the darkness of his cell, fearful that Brusion, or perhaps another person seeking revenge had somehow bribed their way past the guards to extract revenge upon him before the execution.

The small figure stepped quietly towards him. William could vaguely make out the features of his visitor now.

"Miranda?" he whispered, "Miranda, what are you doing here? If your father finds you here..."

"She can't hear or see you, fool!" a familiar voice taunted from the darkest corner of the cell, "Unless I wish it to be so!"

William spun about to face the voice, heart in his throat. The dank cell seemed to fade into the phantom like form of the Beniot family library in which Isabella and he had shared so many evenings together. In confusion, William looked back to Miranda, who stood statue like and beautiful, staring off into space.

"Isabella?" he called out, his blood seeming to turn to ice in his veins.

"Through oblivion he steps," came the voice once more, from one of the great, high backed chairs found in the library, "a fallen angel on the brink of oblivion."

The chair faced away from William, concealing its occupant's identity though William knew the voice well. The voice continued on, reciting the words from one of Lida Beniot's poems, one he had heard before, "Compassion flows, like blood, from his silver tongue. The rose he carries hides a forgotten man. Out of place. Out of time."

"Out of nightmares." William said, finishing the poem.

"Very good." The voice responded as the figure in the chair stirred. In one fluid motion, she rose and stepped around the high backed chair into the candle light of the library, "You have learned your lesson well, lover."

William's body went numb. His mind raced for an avenue of escape, a place to hide from what he saw. There before him stood Isabella Beniot in her burial gown of red trimmed in gold, her decayed body beckoning to him, her ruined mouth, grinning horribly. The beautiful features of her face that he remembered were long rotted away leaving grey, torn flesh hanging loose upon her skull. Her soulless white eyes gazed at him, the irises long since faded. Her raven colored hair hung in matted locks about her head. The smell of rot and rose petals battered William's senses in a sickening aroma of death.

Isabella moved across the room with unnatural motions, her body seeming to glide, her feet dragging the floor.

"So," she spoke through her rotted teeth, "this is your new flesh puppet? Your new meat whore? How shall we kill this one?"

"Isabella," William finally summoned enough courage to speak, "she is but a girl."

"A girl that you chose to be your confidant?" the rotting corpse asked. "Couldn't I have been that for you?"

Isabella hovered before Miranda Winston, staring into her unknowing eyes.

"You professed to love me," Isabella continued, reaching out a withered hand to stroke the girl's wavy brown hair, bringing it forward to her ruined nose and breathing deep of her smell, "Yet, you couldn't bring yourself to tell me the secrets of your past? Of your father? This little thing means so much to you after just a few days that you can confide your darkest secrets to her? Perhaps I should taste of her sweet soul and find out for myself if she is indeed worth your affection."

"Isabella," William pleaded with his dead lover, "Please, she has done nothing but listen to the final testament of a man condemned to die. Leave her be, I beg of you."

Isabella looked over her shoulder, letting her dead gaze fall upon William Bell.

"Her soul seems ready for the harvest." She spat, her purple tongue sliding out from beneath her withered lips, crossing the width of her mouth. She reached out with cold, dead hands, and touched Miranda's face.

"So warm..." she hissed, "Do you think that her warmth can take away my coldness of death for a while, my love?"

"Isabella, no!" he whimpered, finding himself unable to move, his body locked in the same state of motionlessness as Miranda. He wondered if Miranda could see Isabella and prayed silently that she could not. Suddenly, the library faded and William was back in his cell. Miranda was no longer with him, but the corpse of Isabella Beniot stood outside of the bars, looking at him with her milky, dead eyes.

"The game will not end so easily, lover." She warned.

"Isabella, please!" William pleaded, "If ever I meant anything to you, I beg you, leave her be. Soon I will die and this will be over."

"If you were anything to me?" the dead woman's voice rasped, "You...You become another vanishing tear in the eye of my soul."

William stood speechless as Isabella moved her face close to the bars.

"I will raise my hand soon," she continued, her voice a knife across glass, "and wipe... you... away."

One of the guards, a dull look on his face, pushed open the door and entered the room. The living corpse was upon him before he could react. With strength not of this world, she grabbed the guard and rammed his head against the bars of the cell. Brains and skull fragments showered over William Bell as the man's head ruptured like a ripe melon against the iron bars. William's howls of terror went unnoticed as Isabella reached down and took the keys to the cell from the dead guard's quivering body. She slid the key into the lock. William staggered as the sound returned, bearing down upon his senses, spinning inside his head. He was torn away from this vision, sliding back through the seams of reality, back to his earthly Hell.

Chapter 24

William opened his eyes. He lay sprawled upon the wooden floor of his cell, his heart racing, the sounds of the mob outside the jail still calling out in anger, the music from Miranda's playing barely audible over the crowd. His thoughts were a jumbled mess, unsure of what was reality and what was fantasy. His body ached and his neck throbbed. He rolled to his stomach, his face against the wet floor. Why was the floor wet? A salty substance, tasting of iron, was upon his lips. He pushed himself up onto his knees, his hands in the dark puddle. William gasped in fright as he recognized the source of the substance. This was the blood of a dead man. Just outside of the cell, slumped against the bars, was the body of one of the guards. William's last meal of bread and water was set carefully, just within the bars. Blood streaked down the iron bars, leaving a slick, blackish film. Chunks of the guard's brains and bits of skull lay decimated upon the cell floor and there in the lock, just as in the vision, was the key to his cell attached to a ring with another key dangling from it.

William sprang to his feet, sliding in the human sludge, ignoring the screaming pain from his body. *Had Isabella gotten to Miranda yet?* he wondered? As quietly as possible, William reached through the bars and turned the key, unlocking the cell door. He carefully stepped over the guard's body as he racked his brain, searching for a way to escape the building.

He quickly crept to the door which led to the front of the jail. Leaning down and peering through the key hole, William could make out the sheriff, Brusion, and the remaining guard sitting around a table playing some type of card game. William knew that he had no time to waste. He took the candle from the sconce on the wall and returned to his cell. He gathered the straw from his make shift bed and began to scatter it about the cell and then around the outer room, setting it aflame as he did so. William crept to the door, his body trembling with anticipation. This would be his last chance for survival. Patiently, he waited as the fire spread and grew. Only when the smoke from the burning straw and wooden building began to fill the room, did he dare to scream, "Fire! Fire!"

William heard the sound of the men in the other room as they hastily pushed away from their table and stormed towards the entrance leading to his cell. They burst through the door and gazed in disbelief at the flames which now engulfed the cell and much of the room.

"Where's Bell?!" Brusion's voice boomed over the crackle of the flames, as he darted towards the cell. Sheriff Winston spotted the body of the fallen guard amidst the flames.

"Dear God!" he exclaimed as he and the other guard rushed forward in an attempt assist their fallen friend.

Brusion scanned the cell through the thick smoke, hoping to find the burning body of William Bell. None of them noticed the crouching figure hiding behind the door. William sprang from his hiding place and ran through the doorway, into the room where the men had been playing cards. He quickly fastened the door behind him. His hands trembled as he used the stolen keys that had granted him freedom from his cell, to lock it. The sound of the door closing and the locking mechanism engaging sent a panic through the men in the fire filled room as they rushed to the portal, pounding against the heavy wood.

William's thoughts were a blur. If he were to step outside, the mob would tear him to pieces and he had only moments before the trapped men broke through the sturdy door.

"Bell!" bellowed Brusion from inside the burning room, "Bell!" His rage was unquestionable as loud coughs and shouts for help were emitted out by the other men. The smell of burning wood and thick smoke spilled forth from the crack beneath the door. William grabbed a heavy coat from the back of one of the chairs and a brimmed hat from the hook on the wall. The locked door shuddered beneath Brusion's attack, as he battered it with his massive shoulder. William quickly donned the coat and hat and raced out the front of the jail and onto the porch.

Heavy smoke drifted out behind him as he shrieked to the surprised crowd, "The jail is on fire! Help them, they are trapped!" He tossed the keys to the ground as he pushed his way through the villagers. Taking him for one of the guards, the locals paid little attention as many of them scattered to gather buckets of water, while a few of the more brave ones grabbed the keys and ran in to rescue the sheriff and his companions.

William ran through the streets of the town, his mind racing. Isabella was ready to kill again and he knew in his heart that the young girl, Miranda, was to be her next victim. William could hear the sound of Miranda still playing her harp, her melody beckoning to him over the distant

panic of the crowd, leading him to her. *Thank God!*
he thought to himself as he followed the sounds of
her song. As William moved closer to the source of
the music he became aware of the low humming in
his head, the sound again distorting his perception
and drawing him away from Miranda's music. The
dark woods at the town's boarder erupted in
madness. William staggered, a prisoner once more,
but not of the living. He tumbled into the dark
forest, drawn by visions, into the sound, into the
kingdom of the dead, a prisoner of death. William
lay on his back, his eyes to the heavens as reality
collapsed around him. He could see the windows
in the steeple of the church, from high upon its hill.
He could feel the figure with eyes upon him as he
convulsed. In his mind, he could see his Isabella,
watching him.

Chapter 25

Miranda Winston stood from the wooden stool at her harp, done with her playing, hoping that the strange young man who patiently awaited death in her father's jail knew that she was thinking of him. She went across to her bed and pulled back her pillows to reveal the item that she had taken from the jail. As she had left the alley way earlier this evening she had gone back and entered the jail to speak with her father but Landon Taylor had just arrived. The guards, her father, and the man she knew now as Brusion Beniot had accompanied Mister Taylor as he entered the room to confront the caged William Bell, leaving the front of the jail unattended. Setting on the table beside the sickle that was used in the children's murders was a small book with a name inscribed upon it: Lida Beniot. Miranda had heard so much about this book from William's stories that her curiosity wouldn't be denied. She grabbed the small journal from the table and slid it beneath the folds of her gown. When the guards and her father returned with the visibly shaken Landon Taylor the sheriff spoke with her briefly about trivial matters before sending her on her way home. That was hours ago.

Miranda reached down and picked up her new found prize letting her sore finger tips play over the leather bound pages. These pages, pinned by a dying woman, idolized by a dead girl that refuses to stay dead, and carried by a man that had prophetic visions of death. What did these pages hold that were so important to them? She sat down upon her bed, opened the book and started reading the cursed writings of Lida Beniot.

Page after page, Miranda devoured the inner workings of Lida Beniot's mind, spreading out before her on the paper, the driving force behind Isabella Beniot's search for her mother's lost love, taken away too soon by death. She imagined these pages being recited by Isabella to William in the humid gardens behind the Beniot mansion on late summer nights. The poems grew darker as death crept closer to claim Isabella's mother. She could almost feel the despair with which Lida wrote. Miranda skipped about the pages. As the book neared its end, symbolic of the life of Lida Beniot, there were many strange writings, frightening and senseless. Random words and letters, answers to which there seemed to be no questions, dates with no meaning scattered about, and odd drawings that could have been sketched straight from nightmares. Lida's dying process was there, in its entirety. Miranda felt odd, reading the private moments of this woman's demise, witnessing the raw emotion and pain, the anger and delirium, all frozen in time. She flipped to the last page. The last written words of Lida Beniot were barely legible, a sign of her weakening state as her final hours drew to a close.

To the void, I shall take you by the hand.

That was how it ended, how she ended, reaching out to death. She shut the book and sat there on her bed in deep thought.

How painful it must have been for Isabella Beniot as a little girl to watch her mother wilt away. How sad that she remained locked away in that mansion afterwards, sneaking into her mother's room to search for lingering crumbs of her existence to fill the emptiness left by her death. What would drive someone that knew such pain to become what William Bell says she is now? And what was she? A ghost that makes others suffer as she has? A hating spirit of vengeance? What does she want?

Miranda's eyes widened as she realized that in her hands could be the key. William had taken the journal of Lida Beniot on the night that Isabella had died. The journal that was Isabella's most precious and loved belonging. Could this be what was keeping Isabella from leaving this world, anchored to this realm? Was this the source of such torture and devastation? Had William Bell caused this curse and was now spreading it like a disease to any that crossed his path?

The smell of burning timber drifted into Miranda's bedroom carried on the night breeze. She rose from her bed and went to her window which stood half open as she had left it so that William could hear her harp playing. She could hear the yelling of the distant crowd, a continuous murmur of noise. An orange glow lit up the sky and she could see heavy smoke floating upwards from the direction of the jail. Panic filled her heart as she rushed from her room, Lida Beniot's journal grasped firmly in her hand. She raced down the stairs of her house and out into the town streets. As fast as she could, she ran towards the orange glow. She thought of her father and prayed silently that he was safe. Her thoughts jumped to William, she said a prayer for him as well. Could this have been the doing of Isabella Beniot?

Miranda ran the same familiar path to the jail, the same course that she had taken a thousand times or more throughout her childhood. She rounded the corner at the end of the street and saw the jail engulfed in angry flames, spitting and hissing as the structure was destroyed. A line of villagers formed a human chain, passing buckets of water from one person to another, in a futsal attempt to combat the raging fire.

"Father! Father!" she screamed, in a panic, as she ran towards the blaze, "Where is my father?!"

Strong hands grabbed Miranda's wrist and she was spun about to see her father's smut covered face. Miranda fell into his arms tightly hugging him as he crushed her with a strong hug of his own.

"What happened?" she sobbed, "I was so worried for you!"

"Bell." the sheriff said flatly, "He killed one of the guards and then set fire to the jail. When we entered to put out the flames he managed to escape and lock us inside to die. Thomas and several others were able to brave the flames and unlock the door to free us. That fiend, Bell, is loose in our town right now! You must return home at once! Do you hear me, girl? Lock the doors and do not leave! I will come to you once we have Bell. I love you, daughter. Now go!" The sheriff turned to Thomas, who was standing at his side, "Escort her home and stay with her until I arrive."

"Yes, sheriff!" Thomas nodded as he stepped forward to follow Miranda who was already briskly moving towards her home.

Miranda's mind was the victim of a myriad of thoughts. Had William Bell actually committed these heinous acts? Or could it have been the creature that the grandmother of the murdered Taylor children had seen? The murderous red dressed beast that William called Isabella, the killer that William had last seen in the church windows.

Miranda looked up through the smoky night towards the old white church, its upper floor and steeple visible above the tree tops. Was she really there? Possibly watching this carnage unfold? Angry at the world and in search of her mother's journal? Miranda touched the small book, hidden safely away in the folds of her dress. If this Isabella was real, as William and old lady Taylor said, then maybe she could end all of this by returning the book. She could silence this raging spirit and save William as well.

Miranda shifted her eyes to Thomas who was nervously looking about, worried that Bell was in the shadows, ready to spring upon them at any moment.

"Thomas!" she shouted, pointing towards an alley, "Who is that?"

"Stay behind me!" Thomas told Miranda as he stepped forward trembling, his musket at the ready as he approached the dark alley. After scanning the dark passageway for a few long moments Thomas was convinced that the alley was empty.

"Don't worry, dear," he said as he turned back to where Miranda had been, "No one is there."

Thomas lowered his musket again as he turned in circles in the center of the street. He was alone now.

Chapter 26

The sunlight poured down, warm and welcoming, on William Bell as he stood in the empty village streets. He looked about the ghost town and found no signs of life save the small girl with curly brown hair that stood at his side. He looked down at the child's pretty oval shaped face. She was familiar to him but at the same time, a stranger.

"Where is everyone, child?" William spoke to the girl.

Placing a small finger against her lips, the girl motioned for William to be silent.

"They are all dead," she whispered, "and she is coming."

William knelt down before the girl. "Who, child?" he asked in a hushed tone, "Who is coming?"

"The angel." she responded, a sense of fear and sorrow invading her large almond shaped eyes.

"If it is an angel that you await," William said, sensing the tension that had suddenly washed over the child, "then why are you afraid?"

The child looked past William and raised her hand pointing down the street that moments ago was empty. William looked over his shoulder. There it stood, a living doll, or perhaps a marionette that no longer had need for its strings. It had long white robes stirring gently on the wind. Its black hair flowed softly about its head. Its face was non-existent, just a flat, featureless surface that seemed to stare at them with eyes that were not there. The sunlight gleamed off of the overly large sickle that the thing clutched in its hand.

William stood from where he had been kneeling. He reached down and lifted the girl into his arms.

"What's your name, love?" he asked, forcing a smile as he started off down the street, his pace quickening, taking them away from the faceless horror.

"Miranda." the child whimpered, as she buried her face into William's neck, hiding from the thing behind them.

"Please, God! Not again!" William begged, becoming aware that he was in the throes of the sound.

The sound of wooden footsteps striking the street came from behind. It was following them, no, now running behind them! William was now at a full stride, with this faceless angel of doom at his heels. The quiet whimperings of the child battled away the exhaustion as the race for life continued. Chancing a look back over his shoulder, he saw that the hooked blade seemed to be moving ever closer. Sweat poured down his face as fatigue plagued his body. Ahead, William could see a small open door just large enough for the child. Racing death, he thrust the child into her would be salvation and slammed the door closed behind her. The angel doll was upon him now with its scent of death and roses. The faceless angel puppet of Isabella Beniot lashed out with her crooked blade. It vanished again and again into his back, driving him to the ground. The thing upon his back reached around with its sickle blade, sliding it across his throat. A fountain of crimson gushed forward from the wound, spraying across the ground and William Bell prepared to die. His dying eyes were transfixed upon the emotionless mask of hate, as the doll thing rose from his back and stepped to where the child was hidden. William was powerless, his life blood draining freely, the muffled sound of his own heart slowing was in his ears. It was at this point that he realized his error. The structure that he had hastily placed the child in was an upright coffin. A coffin that he had sealed. The faceless angel of death seemed to study the coffin for a moment before setting upon it with primal fury, hacking and stabbing. Blood leaked from the box from the many different holes, dripping down the wooden surface and pooling at the foot of the coffin. William wished to scream, but the gaping tear across his throat would not permit it. His mouth opened and closed, like that of a dying fish, gasping for air that would not come. This is not what he wanted. Not how he should end. The coldness of death crept up his body, engulfing him as his vision faded, dragging him back to oblivion.

Chapter 27

Miranda made her way up the steep twisting road to the old church that overlooked her village. Her heart pounded as she clutched the journal of Lida Beniot, each step taking her closer to the unknown. What if this Isabella was lying in wait within the church? What would she do then? Could she handle the horror of a dead woman walking before her? Would returning the stolen book stop the murderous rampage that had driven Isabella Beniot? She would soon find out.

Miranda walked up the steps to the front of the church, turning back to look at her town below. The fire at the jail had spread to the surrounding structures and it seemed that the entire block was now overtaken with flames, the sky aglow with the orange light.

She made her way to the tall double doors and pushed them open. By the light streaming through the large arching windows, she could make out the two small coffins of the Taylor children near the front of the church, already sealed and awaiting burial the next day now that their father had returned. The smell of death was strong here, even over the perfumes and incense that was being used to mask the odor. Cautiously,

Miranda moved down the aisle towards the coffins, searching each row of pews as she went, fearful of a dead girl that wanted the book that she carried in her white knuckled hands.

Miranda lifted her sleeved arm to her face as she walked between the small coffins, attempting to shield her nose from the smell. A small plaque adorned each lid, with each child's name carved into it. Miranda couldn't help but feel great pity for the children's father. He had lost so much. Soon this nightmare would be behind them all, she hoped. Soon Isabella Beniot will be at rest. Miranda made her way past the old harp that she often played in church, to the stairway that led to the landing on the second floor of the church. It was in those upper windows that William Bell had sworn that he had seen Isabella. She carefully negotiated the steps. Not a sound could be heard within the church walls save the soft footfalls of Miranda Winston.

Miranda moved through the upper floor of the church, fearfully checking each room, each closet, and the areas left for storage, afraid that she may indeed find what she was searching for. Ultimately, she uncovered no signs that the red clad specter from William Bell's tale had ever been there.

The sound of the large double doors slamming closed at the front of the church startled Miranda. She looked anxiously down the hall toward the landing and the stairway. She took a few steps forward, listening. *Was it the wind blowing the doors closed*, she wondered? Two more loud crashes followed, echoing throughout the empty church.

"Hello?" she called out, her voice not at all as strong and confident as she had hoped it would sound, "Is anyone there?"

Silence was the reply as she crept onto the landing overlooking the worship hall below. The doors at the rear of the church were indeed closed now. Miranda moved to the stairway and began her descent. She eyed the bottom of the stairs, fearful of shadows and the unknown beyond her limited view. As she came to the bottom of the stairway her heart seemed to cease beating. William Bell's story came rushing back to her with haunting clarity. The scent of rose petals overpowered the smell of the dead. Between the children's coffins which now stood on end, the lids ripped away to expose the rotting corpses, was the gaunt form of a woman wearing a long red gown trimmed in brilliant gold. Her long black hair hung in matted locks about her head. Her ruined mouth trembled from out of the shadows as she stood there, seemingly admiring her handy work, a farming sickle clutched in her hand.

Terror overtook Miranda as she stumbled back up the stairway, the journal forgotten, tucked away in the folds of her dress. The animated corpse of William Bell's lover turned her attention towards Miranda Winston now. Miranda screamed as she fled up the stairs, the slap of dead flesh on wood alerting her that Isabella was at her heels. Fear took control of Miranda's body, her movements suddenly slow and clumsy. The very fabric of her dress seemed to come alive, twisting about her, slowing her flight from the dead. Miranda felt a cold hand claw at her foot as she reached the top of the stairs, causing her to lose her footing and sending her tumbling to the floor with a painful thud. Dazed, she attempted to pick herself up, to continue her race for her life, but Isabella was already upon her. Black hair hung down over Miranda as Isabella's body, cold and rigid, fell against her back. The smell of a weeks old corpse caused her to gag in repulsion.

"I am mad, I am mad!" Miranda screamed from her stomach, the dead woman on top of her, her mind refusing to accept what was ravaging her senses.

"A bit of madness is good for the soul." the thing hissed into her ear, its icy breath sending chills throughout her body. One of Isabella's hand grasped Miranda's hair, arching back her neck, preventing her from escaping. The blade of the sickle carried in the thing's other hand slid up and down Miranda's body perversely.

"So," it rasped, "shall I show you why William loved me best?"

"Please," Miranda pleaded through broken sobs, "please just leave me be! Go back to hell where you belong!"

"What do you think you are to him, angel whore?" Isabella raged.

Then Isabella was tearing at Miranda's dress with her curved blade, cutting her body, violating her. The corpse of a dead woman was stripping away her dignity before bringing her over to the land of the dead. Isabella's flesh was cold and lifeless against her. Miranda squirmed and twisted over onto her back, pawing at the sagging dead face that stared down at her. Isabella cackled with delight at the struggles of her helpless victim.

"Tonight," she growled, her voice barely human, "I will flay your soul and feast upon it!"

Isabella's tongue flicked out, lapping at the fresh blood on her blade.

Miranda shrieked, lashing out, her fingers catching in the monster's matted hair. As she struggled, the entire rotting face and scalp of Isabella Beniot pulled free, falling to the floor beside her, leaving her looking up into the crazed eyes of William Bell.

Chapter 28

William looked down at the shaking form of Miranda Winston, crying and screaming beneath him. He looked, confusingly, at the bloody sickle in his hand. He pushed himself up from the girl as she scurried out from under him. He looked down at the red gown that he wore, trimmed in gold. Isabella's mother's favorite dress. Isabella's burial gown. William dropped the sickle, his eyes wide in terror, tears pouring down his face as he looked down at the shriveled face of Isabella Beniot on its bed of matted black hair, discarded like some terrible mask from his worst nightmare.

"No!No!No!" he screamed as he collapsed to the floor, tearing the dress from his body, the pounding of the sound strong in his head, pushing away rational thought. He saw visions now.

He saw the university that he so loved, but it seemed different. Williamsburg, Virginia? Was that where it was? No, not a university, but a hospital for the mentally insane. He could see the gate in his mind. How many years did he spend there? Professor Winkler? The one in whom he entrusted so many of his dark secrets from his past, what of him? Not a professor. No. He saw him, now, in his white coat. He was a doctor. The doctor that hounded him relentlessly day and night with questions and tests, promising to cure him, but nothing was wrong with him. The visions continued to flood into his consciousness, as if a mental dam had burst. He remembered the day that Professor Winkler, no, Doctor Winkler had told him of his mother's impending death, but did that happen? No, it didn't. William remembered now how he escaped the hospital and fled back to his home, breaking into his house and sneaking to his aging mother's room where she lay dying. She wasn't dying. That was his mind playing tricks again, but didn't she die? Yes, of course she did, when William placed the pillow over her face as she slept and smothered her. Why? Why would he do that? William's father had come in to gloat about his mother's death, about ending her life, but what William saw was the old man trying to pull him off of his mother. William pushed the old man back into the hall and hurled him down the stairs, stomping the old man's skull with his boots as he fled from his home amid the screams from the servants.

What was happening to him? William screamed and writhed, naked on the floor as Miranda pulled herself to her feet. Limping and bleeding from numerous cuts, she fled from the naked madman.

Inside William's head the visions continued. He saw the body of Doctor Winkler tossed in a ditch along the road that led to the University...*no, hospital!* He was dead? He recalled fleeing to New Orleans and how the visions stopped once he found Isabella, how she made everything alright. They were going to flee to Paris and she loved him, didn't she? She fled from her home with him, didn't she? How did she die? He remembered attacking his father in the streets of New Orleans, but that couldn't be. His father was dead. He had attacked Isabella. He was so sorry, sick from it. She had tried to leave him that night. He remembered her getting out of bed, sick and beaten. She was going to leave him alone. She was going to betray him like the rest when they had him locked away all of those years ago. Without her, the vision would return. That night she died. He knew that he was lost. The visions started again, almost with her last breath. She hated him now and would not stay dead. She would herald the visions, the sound. She would usher doom to his doorstep. He loved her so. She couldn't be dead. Not his Isabella.

He remembered slipping into the Beniot family burial yard late in the night after Isabella's funeral, after the earlier fight with her family and her following interment. In the darkness of that night he clawed into the muddy earth until he reached her coffin. He wiped away the mud covering the window and smiled at his lost love through the dirty glass. He remembered tearing open the lid with the aid of a farming sickle that he had stolen from one of the tool sheds located on the property. He pulled Isabella's rigid body from the box and pushed it out of the grave and onto the ground. He took her into the wooded countryside where he carefully slid the sickle blade beneath the skin of her jaw, gently carving away her face and scalp. William packed away her favorite red gown, trimmed in gold, along with her mother's journal, placing them in the saddle bag of his stolen horse. He kissed the skinned face of his dead lover before hiding it away with the sickle in another pouch. Then he fled New Orleans forever.

William screamed louder as the revelations became more than he could bear. He saw himself as Isabella Beniot, rampaging through a convent, slaughtering any who crossed his path and burning it to the ground. He saw himself murdering the children on the Taylor farm beneath the light of the moon, and his horse galloping away, spooked, with the sickle and Lida Beniot's journal in the saddle bag. He could recall retreating up to this church, hiding Isabella's dress and disembodied face in the upper level and staring down over the village, a predator of men.

He saw himself grabbing the guard through the bars as he leaned forward to set down his last supper and pulling forward again and again, smashing the man's skull until his brains leaked out. He recalled setting the cell afire and sneaking out, locking the others within and grabbing Isabella's sickle from the table as he fled, hiding it beneath his stolen coat, but it wasn't him. Not since New Orleans. It was Isabella! She rode into his psyche on the waves of the sound, using his body to murder. He was as much a tool to her as the sickle that she used to claim her victims.

"Miranda!!!!" he screamed as he rolled to his knees grabbing the curved blade from the floor. He remembered the vision from earlier, the one where the faceless angel of Isabella had killed the girl named Miranda. "Isabella's will must be carried out!" he yelled as he rose on unsteady legs and began stalking the church, searching for his offering to his dead lover.

Chapter 29

Miranda pushed forward on her wounded legs as fast as her body would allow. Cries of pain came with each anguished step as she hunted for a hiding place from the raving lunatic that was screaming her name. She opened the door that led to the steeple and stepped inside. She could hear the sound of William Bell's bare feet on the floor as he hurled himself towards her, a deranged scream emitting from him. Just in time, she fastened the door and barred it from within as William's weight slammed against it, causing the wood to pop and splinter under the impact. Miranda screamed at the man through the door.

"William, just leave me alone, please!" she begged.

William Bell stared at the door and listened to the familiar voice from within.

"You listened to me, today, while I was a prisoner, wishing to hear my story. Don't you wish to hear how it ends?" William yelled as he set upon the door with the sickle, driving the blade into the wood again and again.

Miranda screamed as she turned, looking for a means to escape. She grabbed the rope to the church bells and pulled vigorously with all of her might. The church bells rocked back and forth, ringing and chiming, deafening inside the steeple where Miranda hid. The sounds of the ringing bells seemed to deepen William's madness as he hacked away at the door with a new found frenzy.

Down in the village the church bells sounded over the land drawing the attention of the townspeople. Those fighting the fire stopped and looked towards the church upon the hill. Who would be ringing those bells at this time? Thomas ran up to Sheriff Winston, out of breath.

"Sheriff! It's Miranda, she vanished on the way to your home!" he spoke, regretfully.

The sheriff looked to the church on the hill as the bells tolled.

"Miranda!" he yelled as he broke to a stride, heading down the road to the path that led to the church.

Brusion had been searching the village, hunting his sister's killer. He cursed himself for being taken by surprise in the jail like some commoner. It wasn't like him to be so reckless. The sound of the church bells suddenly ringing drew his attention, *was this to alert everyone of the fire?* If so, the warning had come very late. No, this seemed to be something else. Brusion drew his pistol and began running towards the church and the furiously ringing bells.

It didn't take the young soldier long to cover the distance to the church. He ran up the steps of the church, pistol in one hand and a torch in the other. With one well-placed kick, he gained entry into the structure and was immediately greeted by madness. Two dead children stood in their coffins, facing him, near the altar of the church. He could hear a loud commotion, between the tolling of the bells. Coming from upstairs, he could make out the sound of a woman screaming and the pounding of metal against wood. Brusion ran to the stairway, his powerful legs propelling him up the steps three at a time. In moments, he was crossing the landing towards the sounds of the screams and the ringing bells. In his haste, he did not notice his sister's burial gown lying crumpled on the floor. As he turned the corner into the hallway Brusion could see William Bell, his back to him, standing naked, his families sickle in his hand. The sheriff's distraught daughter could be seen through the gaping hole that Bell had hacked into the wooden door. William turned slowly to face Brusion, an insane gleam in his eyes. With a crazed shriek, William Bell hurled himself down the hallway towards Brusion Beniot, his sickle, slick with blood, gleaming in the torch light. Brusion stepped back onto the landing as Bell rounded the corner, his curved blade ready to strike. Brusion raised his pistol and fired. The explosion of fire and gunpowder filled the room as William Bell collapsed to the floor in a heap. Smoke drifted up from Bell's body as Brusion holstered his pistol and drew his knife. The young soldier moved cautiously toward the facedown body of his sister's killer. He stepped over the still form of William Bell and approached the sheriff's daughter, still barricaded behind the heavily damaged door.

"It's over, girl." he said trying to calm Miranda, "He is dead. William Bell is dead!"

Brusion smiled at his words. His sister could now rest in peace. Miranda's scream shook Brusion from his distracting thoughts. He turned to find the maniacal William Bell lunging up from the ground, a bloody wound in his upper left chest still smoking. The blade from the sickle penetrated Brusion's abdomen just under the ribs, scraping the inside of his rib cage as it tore up through his insides. The sudden excruciating pain caused the big man to drop his knife and torch. Brusion's massive hands clasped around Bell's neck as the two men staggered about the landing. Miranda quickly unbarred the door to her hiding place and ran down the hall toward the fighting men, hoping to slink by them. She made it onto the landing, but the battling men blocked her escape. William pulled and ripped wildly with the sickle, tearing organs inside of the large man. Brusion yelped in agony as he squeezed tightly, hoping to break Bell's neck before he died. Brusion lost his footing and fell backwards, tumbling towards one of the large windows. The blade tore free as he crashed through the glass and toppled out the window, landing lifeless on the ground below. Brusion Beniot was dead. William stared out the broken window at the man that had long tormented him, lying dead on the ground. In the distance he could see torches approaching.

"Isabella?" William called over his shoulder, the sound buzzing in his ears, "Don't worry, my love. I'll finish this for you."

Miranda looked down and saw the knife that Brusion had dropped. She knelt quietly to pick it up, but William Bell was there slapping it from her hand. She cried out as he slammed her against the wall, her head bouncing off the wood. His hand was upon her face opening her mouth reaching for her tongue. Miranda's terrible screams filled the church as he tore her tongue from her mouth. She collapsed to the floor, blood flooding from her mouth and through her hands as she groped for the wound that she couldn't reach, chocking on her own fluids. William gathered up the red dress and pulled it over Miranda's head. He walked across the landing and retrieved the torch that Brusion had dropped. The flames had already charred part of the floor, smoke rising from the burnt area, threatening to combust. He crossed back over to Miranda and pulled her hair back, exposing her face.

"We are cleansed in these flames." he said and held the torch to her face, melting away her soft skin. Miranda howled in unequaled agony as the smell of her burning skin filled the landing. William, unconcerned, tossed the torch across the floor. He then lovingly picked up the skin mask of the dead woman and placed it on Miranda Winston, pressing it, melding it with her burnt

flesh as she vomited blood through her new mouth.

A strange smile spread across his face. "My love!" he said, his face like that of a child receiving a long wanted toy, "You have come back to me!"

Chapter 30

The sheriff and several of the villagers had arrived just in time to see Brusion Beniot fall from the upper window of the church, landing on the church lawn, dead, his intestines hanging from his body. Sheriff Winston raced to the body of the young man.

"Damn it!" he cursed as he turned and ran towards the front of the church. Two of the villager stood frozen with fear at the open doors. The sheriff ran up the steps to see the two dead children standing in their coffins and up on the landing was the bloody and naked form of William Bell standing before a woman in a red dress, trimmed in gold, her matted black hair framing her sagging dead face with blood flowing from its mouth. This was the thing that the Old woman Taylor had seen. This was Isabella Beniot.

"Sheriff!" one of the men said, summoning enough nerve to talk, "Those things have already killed a trained soldier! What chance do we have against the likes of these demons?"

From the landing, Miranda Winston saw through the eye slits of dead flesh, her father standing in the doorway of the church. She turned and with all of the strength that her weakened could muster, she raced for the stairs.

Sheriff Winston's eyes grew wide and goose flesh rose all over his body as the dead thing in the red dress ran down the stairs, unleashing an unholy moan. It ran out into the worship hall and between the two standing coffins and down the aisle, straight towards him. Sheriff Winston found the courage to step across the threshold and pull both doors shut. Then the thing was upon them, snatching and pounding at the wooden doors, screaming in its horrible gargled voice.

"Help me bar these doors!" screamed the sheriff. "We can't let these things out!"

Several more men moved forward to help hold the doors, while others went to find something to create a barrier against the seemingly demonic things inside.

"What are we going to do?" cried one of the men, panic in his voice. The sheriff looked about as he held the doors against the monster inside, trying to get out. He could see more of the townspeople heading towards the church, having abandoned fighting the hopeless fire in town. *That was it!*

"Gather your torches! Throw brush under the windows! We will burn them here and purge the world of their evil!" shouted the sheriff.

The villagers spread out to accomplish the tasks that were set before them. Inside the church, William Bell walked down the stairs to his lover, carrying the sickle in one hand and Lida Beniot's journal in the other.

"Isabella," he called to Miranda Winston, who had collapsed with her back against the door, "It's not like you to leave this unattended, my dear. Are you feeling well?"

Miranda stared at the naked madman approaching her through the eye holes of Isabella Beniot, barely conscious from the pain, unable to speak. William knelt before Miranda and placed the journal and sickle on the floor beside him. Stroking the tangled black hair of Isabella, he smiled genuinely at the ruined face as he spoke, "So beautiful."

He took her by the hand as he rose to his feet, drawing her gently to hers.

"Come my sweet, Isabella," he spoke calmly, "let us go drink wine and talk of Paris and our future children, let us laugh and argue, kiss and make love as we used to. I have missed you so much. Your voice in my head just wasn't enough."

Miranda rose to her feet, one hand in William Bell's, the other wrapped around the handle of the sickle that he had carried. With a defiant scream, Miranda attacked William Bell. The curved blade of the sickle hacked into his bare back again and again as he fell to the floor. He looked down the aisle at the children standing in the upright coffin, just as in his vision. Isabella Beniot was at his back just as in his vision. The cold blade slid around his neck and across his throat, just as in his vision. William Bell's blood spilled across the church floor in great amounts as his mouth gasped open and closed like a fish out of water. His eyes focused on the dead children in front of him as his world began to grow dark for the final time. He forced a smile at the dead little girl that he was sure was staring at him. He swore that he heard his Isabella, softly beckoning to him, welcoming him home. The sound was finally silent.

Outside the villagers were tossing torches into the brush piles that had been assembled around the church. The sheriff watched through the window as the dead woman attacked William Bell and slaughtered him. He wondered if Bell had been telling the truth the entire time? Had he truly wanted to stop the demonic force that had finally killed him? Maybe he had been innocent, but none of that mattered now. He had to end this unholy creature that had killed so many. Isabella Beniot must die for good this night, for the safety of the people in his community, for the safety of his beloved daughter Miranda. The hot flames rose in a raging whirlwind of fire around the structure. The fire spread quickly, climbing up the steeple and licking at the sky. From inside the burning church, came the familiar sound of a beautifully played harp, the song of an angel, Miranda's song, which lasted until the flames themselves finally drowned out the sound. The sheriff wept.

Epilogue

In the dark woods, watching the smoldering remains of the hill top church, a figure stood with raven black hair. Her soulless eyes gleamed with unnatural vigor as she straightened the folds of her long red dress which was trimmed in golden threads. She smiled with satisfaction as she placed the small journal to her chest and turned to begin her long walk home, back to hell.

About the Author

Howard Boling is an author, artist, and poet. He developed a flare for dark tales and macabre, which transcended into his storytelling and artworks. He has authored several poetry books and provided illustrations for children's books. He currently resides in Northern Mississippi with his wife and children.

Laurel Rose Publishing

Laurel Rose Publishing is an independent publishing company located in North Mississippi. The company was created as a way for unknown authors to get published and get help in marketing their works. If you are interested in publishing a book and want to know how you can do so contact us at www.laurelrosepublishing.com.

Other Books by Howard Boling

Poetry Books:

Hell's Castaway by Howard Boling

A Random Spread of Bones by Howard Boling

Strained Horizons by Howard Boling

Children's Books:

Loralai The Lonely by Chad R Martin & Howard Boling

Stanley's Lost Gift by Chad R Martin & Howard Boling